The First

THE ELITUS SAGA

by

S.H. Reynolds

Published by

Onyx & Amethyst LLC

ESTD 2025

Book Cover by Onyx & Amethyst Designs

1 edition 2025

Dedication

For all the women that can relate to the women of Elitus.
The ones who trained to be weapons but were born to be more.
For every girl who was told her strength was a threat, her ambition a flaw, and that emotions make you weak.
For those who were silenced, sidelined, or used and still stood.
This is for all the Masons, the Andys, the Myas, and the Kates.
For the girls who shattered ceilings with combat boots, sharp tongues, and softer hearts, they weren't afraid to protect.
For the ones who didn't want to be saved, because they became the reckoning instead.
You were never too much.
The world was simply too small.

This story discusses topics that could trigger certain audiences. Topics include domestic abuse, mental health, violence, sex, underage drinking, drug use, profanity, verbal abuse, and physical assault.

CONTENTS

ONE

Alex

I sit at the desk I outgrew a decade ago—dust on the surface, old notebooks left behind like artifacts of a life I vaguely remember. The chair creaks under my weight. My knees hit the underside. The desk, this room, belongs to a version of me that no longer fits.

Downstairs, my family lingers over dessert, laughter echoing through the walls. Soon, I'll join them. The auditorium and my graduation are waiting. I've been training at the Academy since it opened. My class, Generation One, are the first to graduate. At twenty-one, I am no longer just a student—I'm an adult, an operative, a leader in the Elitus community. A Wight, enhanced through Agent X, a serum designed in a lab. Trained to kill before I could drive.

I close my eyes. I need a second. One last breath before I cross a line I can't return from. The room smells of the same clean linen, paper, and a light scent of lemon from our housekeeper's cleaner. But it doesn't feel like mine. Not anymore.

Photos line the walls—frozen moments of a life I barely had time to live. Holidays, staged smiles, official Elitus functions disguised as family events. The annual Winter Ball. The Gauntlet Spring Tournament.

But some are real; the one from the Palace trip, right after Kennedy was born. The sunset behind us all, tan and grinning. Kennedy, a bundle in Maria's arms, my father standing behind her steady and unwavering. Back then, we looked relaxed. Happy, even.

I can't help but wonder when our last actual vacation was? Minus Elitus? When we were a family. Blended, complicated, but normal.

Elitus moved me into the dorms when I was ten. Not because I wanted to go, but because powers similar to mine—combat-class, high threat—require structure. Control. Limits.

And Elitus thrives on control.

From the outside, foliage and fences hide the campus. The Elitus Campus stretches in every direction; a classified government compound that includes research centers, offices, labs, the Academy, dorms, residential housing, and a training center. But beneath the canopy of trees and curated stillness, it's a machine.

My father's house sits on the far edge. Calvin and Mom live two doors down. The entire Elitus Board lives on this block. Our subdivision is on the west side, constantly monitored and maintained. The perfect illusion of privacy. Far enough away to pretend we live a normal life. Too close to believe it.

It spans thousands of acres, masked as farmland and forest. A city masquerading as a campus, every inch humming with deliberate design. Built for one reason: control.

Illusion envelopes the civilian zones, meant for non-combat families. Cookie-cutter homes, clipped lawns, cheerful mailboxes; with surveillance at every corner.

Downstairs, the familiar chaos seeps through the floorboards; Kennedy's giggles, my brothers' deep voices arguing about football, my sisters catching Mason up on everything she missed. Somewhere in the kitchen, pots clang, and cabinet doors shut with purpose; Dad talks strategy with my step-dad Calvin, while Mom and Maria reset the room behind them. That's the rhythm of this house: noise, movement, recovery.

We're not just a blended family—we're a tactical unit disguised as one. Nine Kids. Two Couples. Not all of us are blood related; no white picket fences for us, but somehow, it works.

My parents divorced when I was two and married their new partners before I could form any genuine memories of them being together. But they showed up and built something for our future. They remained friends and made a family despite everything.

And every one of them bleeds Elitus.

My gaze lands on a photo of Pepe and me. Dr. Mason, Maria's father, our grandfather, and the Patriarch of Elitus; he is the man who built this world, not with love, but with a vision.

The house may be full tonight, but he's everywhere in it: on the walls, in the protocol, in the pressure stitched into my spine. Not all legacies are made of family photos and birthday parties.

Elitus started as a whisper—an off-the-books experiment buried beneath layers of government black ops. Funded by slush funds, pushed through under the guise of national defense. No oversight. No accountability. A singular mission: build a stronger soldier.

The threat was real—foreign programs racing to perfect their version of a super soldier, and the U.S. couldn't afford to fall behind. Pepe was the head of the division put in charge of it. He recruited my father right out of college, and everyone else who sits on the Elitus board, including my stepfather, Calvin.

Pepe led the charge through the use of science: genetic engineering, chemical enhancements, and advanced psychological conditioning.

The first iteration of Agent X was never meant to create children. It was supposed to enhance adult soldiers—fast-track evolution. But the results were... unstable, inconsistent, lethal.

Then they discovered its true potential.

Not as a booster. But as a blueprint.

In vitro, the serum reshaped everything—neurology, bone structure, muscle mass, energy regulation, and brainwave capacity. The first successful generation wasn't recruited. We were conceived.

Thirty-five years later, Elitus is still running; stronger, sharper, deeper underground.

And us?

We're called Wights. In declassified files, black ops dockets, whispers between the alphabet agencies.

The name started as a joke, "right combination of genes to make a weapon." Then someone ran with it, and it became an acronym, Weaponized Individuals Genetically Heightened through Technology. And it stuck.

But it fits. We are weapons. Instruments of war wrapped in human skin. Ghosts in the night, hidden, powerful, dangerous, unseen until it's too late.

Our primary function, once combat-enabled, is to run contracts and missions.

Missions come down from the top. Assignments are to be carried out, no names, no questions, just skill sets, powers, and targets.

We were built for this, born for it.

Whether we want it or not.

The weight of our history presses on my spine until I can't sit still anymore. I push back from the desk. The chair groans under me, legs scraping against the floor. A reluctant farewell. I hear Kennedy's voice ringing through the floorboards again, calling my name. It breaks something loose in my chest.

It's time to step out of the memory of my childhood and into everything I was made for.

They call me the First.

I didn't ask for that title, but it hangs over everything. Missions, conversations, even dinner. The title sits heavy on my shoulders, heavier than usual tonight.

Pepe may have built the vision, the Elitus organization. But my father made it real.

Being Robert Clarke's son means the expectations aren't just high, they're institutional. He's the main scientist on Elitus, who helped to develop enhancements and identified success in vitro, the mind that shaped the program for training and development. The hand that fine-tuned every iteration.

And me? I've spent my whole life trying to prove I was worthy of the blueprint. Following every rule. Carrying the name like it's sacred.

With one last look at the room—my childhood in frames and faded posters—I leave it behind, for good.

Downstairs, the house is alive and animated.

Kennedy barrels into me before I've cleared the bottom step. Full of tulle and glitter, all wild eyes, and smiles. She shows off her dress, spinning until the skirt flares. I scoop her up with one arm, tickling her ribs until she squeals. She's supposed to be in bed, but nobody says no to Kennedy.

I hand her off to RJ, who catches her mid-spin like it's choreographed. She wraps her little arms around his neck, still giggling.

I scan the room. Everyone's here; parents, siblings, all except one.

Mason.

I spot her through the sliding glass doors, standing alone on the balcony. I nod to my father, a silent promise, and step outside.

The balcony doors whisper shut behind me. Evening air curls around my collar—cool, steady.

Mason leans against the railing like she owns the horizon. The sunset lights her up from behind, setting her hair ablaze in deep mahogany, burgundy and ember-red. Waves spill down her back, soft and wild. She's a perfect blend of Maria, Robert, and Agent X.

She looks every bit the independent eighteen-year-old, wearing a midnight black, off-the-shoulder body-con dress that hugs every damn curve she has. I shake my head. It's got Maria written all over it. Maria never curbed Mason's flair for style, and since Mason is cut from the same cloth as her mother, her sultry beauty comes naturally.

Mason senses me before I speak, turning just enough to smirk—sharp, knowing, annoyingly smug. "Nervous?" She teases, voice light, eyes dangerous. Sapphire and violet, impossible and unmistakable.

I adjust the collar of my suit jacket, buying myself a second. "No, I'm good. It's about time, honestly. I've earned this."

"Oh, please. Besides, Kate's doing enough worrying for all four of you," she says, rolling her eyes.

I reach over and ruffle her hair as if we're kids again. She swats my hand, scowling, but a smile tugs at her lips anyway. There's pride in her eyes, even if she'd never admit it out loud. "You will be the first one up there," she reminds me.

"I'm aware," I tell her, watching her as she looks out over the grounds. The rolling hills behind our parents' house stretch out as far as the eye can see.

"You know they only call you the First because it sounds better than saying test subject one, right?" She jokes. She should know; after all, she was an incident in their theory. An unplanned conception, one that was full of random variables, but proved to be extraordinary from a genetic and success standpoint of the program. Although most of Elitus would never admit that.

Mason isn't like the rest of us. She never has been.

At eighteen, she's all sharp lines and sharper instincts—born to fight, bred to defy. She shed "Mia" like a skin the day she turned eight and declared herself for combat. From that moment on, she was just Mason.

"You shouldn't be nervous either. Your time is coming," I tell her, nudging her shoulder. "You'll be throwing your own grad party before we know it."

Her grin returns, fierce and wicked. "Obviously. But I'm not nervous about that. I'm nervous because if I have to spend one more night locked inside this house, I will commit actual violence."

I wince. "That's what happens when you and Charley cram twenty people in your room and throw a party. Did you think no one would notice?"

"It was a dare." Her tone is unapologetic.

"You're lucky you didn't burn the place down."

"I didn't." She tosses her hair over her shoulder. "You're welcome."

I narrow my eyes, already bracing for her next jab. She tilts her head, smile sharpening. Then she lands the hit.

"Andy sure liked it."

My heart stumbles. I try not to react. Try to shove the name back where I buried it. But Mason sees too much.

Andrea Parrish. Her name alone scrapes against the inside of my chest.

Heat and guilt. Want and regret. All tangled in one sharp breath, I can't quite let go.

She's younger than I am, but you'd never know it. Andy walks into a room as if it owes her something—like every set of eyes should follow, and most of the time, they do.

At nineteen, she's all chaos and confidence. Combat-class.

She parties until she forgets who she is. Drinks until the rules blur. And often, someone has to pull her out before she crashes.

Lately, that someone has been me. Even when I know I shouldn't, even when it hurts.

I don't chase alcohol highs. I don't get sloppy. That's never been me.

But lately, I've been chasing her. Wondering where she is and who she's with. If she's safe. I'm drawn to her. And as much as I know Andy is a weakness I can't afford, I can't avoid her.

The more I try to, the more I orbit around her.

Mason has been watching this train wreck in slow motion for years.

I shove her shoulder, harder this time, like that'll undo the look she gives me. She laughs triumphantly.

"Andy should know her limits," I mutter. "And you shouldn't egg her on. Not everyone can hang like you do."

Mason grins, her signature smirk in place. "Exactly. That's what makes it fun." Shaking my head at her, I maneuver her back inside, where our loud but loving family awaits.

"Max and Calvin are outside," RJ says, stepping back from the coat closet. "Engines are running, let's move."

I help Mom—Joanne—into her light jacket, smoothing the fabric over her shoulders. Her smile is watery but determined. She's trying not to cry; I move fast before she breaks.

"Let's go," I say, steering the rest toward the door.

Mason is already halfway there. She strides outside and straight into Max's gravity. He's leaning against the SUV, one hand in his pocket. His dark chestnut hair falls just above his brow, framing a face built of sharp cheekbones, a strong jawline, and lips that hold a smirk aimed at our sister. His dark sapphire eyes, the same base gem color as Mason's.

They're half-siblings, but anyone watching would guess otherwise. They share the same smile, the same coloring, the same eyes, and the same sarcastic nature.

We may not share blood, but Max and I were raised side by side. And we've perfected the same Big Brother aura.

"Ready to escape?" he asks her, voice low, lips twitching.

Mason sticks her tongue out. Full brat mode, unbothered and bold. Max was at the party that got her grounded, and as usual, he somehow walked away clean while she took the fall.

It's always been this way. Mason's the default scapegoat. Although used to it, it is still unfair to her. The rules for Mason and the girls are stricter. They do it under the guise of keeping them safe and controlled. I think it just makes them rebel more.

We get into the cars, the buzz in the air almost tangible. Mason slides into the Escalade's middle row, flanked by our sisters, Aimee, and Mya. Max and I climb in front, while our other siblings split off. RJ and Kennedy head with Dad and Maria, and my half-brothers, Jonah and Ryan, go with their dad, Calvin, and Mom.

The road to the auditorium is short, but the tension in the car runs long.

"I still think they should have let Aimee out," Mason mutters from the back, loud enough to stir the pot. "It's practically a sanctioned event tonight at the dorms."

Max laughs. "Kyle threatened to sneak off campus and get trashed if Ames didn't approve it. She caved in under five minutes."

"Still sucks I'm stuck," Aimee huffs. She still lives with Mom and Calvin, since she isn't in combat training. Then she adds, low but lethal, "Next year."

It sounds like a threat. And knowing Aimee, it probably is.

We pull up to the auditorium, sleek and silent like a monolith carved from shadow. Black glass wraps around the exterior. The car's warmth evaporates the moment we step out. Outside, everything sharpens, the reality of the night setting it.

Inside, the light is low and reverent, deep purples and obsidian reflections dancing across polished marble floors. Everything glows. The entire building is holding its breath.

A cool blast of climate control hits as we step through the doors. The air smells sterile. Sanitized. Standard Elitus.

But tonight?

It hums with tension. Anticipation.

Calvin walks in with Mom, their hands laced. She peels off to hug me—tight, emotional, and reflective.

"I'm so proud of you," she whispers, squeezing my middle. "Katherine mentioned they'll be organizing a formal social next year, something bigger, when Gen Two goes."

Mason doesn't even flinch, but her mouth twitches. Mom catches it. "I know you throw your own thing, but just—keep it low-key tonight, okay?"

"Low key's my specialty," Mason lies smoothly, throwing an arm around Mom's shoulders. She doesn't respond. Just gives her that dangerous little smile that says she knows everything.

Everyone splits off, and just like that, the safety net unravels. One by one, we step into our roles; RJ, Mya, and Aimee peel off toward the Gen Four section. Mason and Max disappear down the aisle towards the Gen Threes and Gen Twos, and I make my way to the stage.

Deep-violet drapes line the platform. Platinum lights cut harsh angles across the black flooring. There are no caps and gowns at this ceremony.

Just medallions.

Black onyx and platinum. Weighted. Cold. Designed by my father as more than decoration. They're a message, a symbol of Elitus and Wights.

I sit in the metal chair onstage, the seat unyielding beneath me. My spine locks straight, fingers resting on my thighs.

I try to focus. But then I see her: Andy.

She's sitting in my line of sight, like the universe is in on the joke. Her hair falls in loose blond waves past her shoulders. The black sequin halter dress, sleek and understated until the light hits it. When she moves, it comes alive with a shimmer. It makes her even more beautiful, impossible to look away from.

She looks magnificent. She's not looking at me, which gives me a second, just one, to look at her without consequences.

But I don't need to see her to feel her. Her energy always finds me, even when she's across the room, when she's supposed to be untouchable. Two forces pull us together.

I told myself I'd stopped wanting her months ago, that we were just a bad idea waiting to happen. Then I see her laughing, beautiful, and energetic, and I forget how to lie to myself.

I can't have her. Elitus doesn't allow in-house relationships. Especially not for those being groomed to lead.

Besides that, she is my best friend's twin. Close with my sisters. She is wild, carefree, and untamed. A soldier under my command, and a year out from graduation.

Her focus needs to be on her training. Not on me.

For myself, I must focus on what comes next, working within Elitus, driving the program forward.

I've told myself it's for her safety. For me.

Rules are rules, and I'm supposed to follow them. Lead by example.

But tonight, with her this close?

The rules feel a lot like chains.

Andy

I'm not even looking for him, but the second he walks in. I feel it.

A shift in the air; a change in gravity. I spot Alex breaking from his family, walking toward the stage like he belongs there. My chest tightens, a fist closing around my lungs.

He always looks good—clean lines, calm expression, that impossible mix of discipline and quiet power—but tonight?

Tonight, he's lethal. Maybe it's the light. Or the suit. Or the way he carries every inch of power, as if it was forged into his bones.

Whatever it is, I try my hardest not to stare at him, but I can't look away.

Alex is always a contradiction—polished and pressed in suits during class or with Elitus. Then there is the combat weapon, black fatigues, military-issue boots, commanding, a living weapon. Danger wrapped in a blond-haired, seawater-blue-eyed package.

My fingers twitch in my lap. I need something, anything, to dull this fire. Alcohol works sometimes. It's not about getting drunk—it's about quieting everything else.

We use it to dull the buzz of our power that always simmers under the surface. But tonight, I know I shouldn't drink. I need to stay sharp and in control.

Alex Clarke is off-limits; he is Elitus' golden boy. The rule follower, leader, Robert's son; the oldest and the First child of Elitus.

He wears responsibility like a badge and carries everyone else's weight without ever asking for help.

And me? I am chaos-wrapped in combat boots. A combat-enabled wight, one of Mason's best friends.

One of the few females demanding combat status, I'm the one who knows how to get into trouble and never apologizes for it.

My stomach knots tightly, something molten and wicked curling low in my belly as he takes his place on the stage. I should focus on the ceremony—its significance.

This is his moment. After years of brutal training, relentless discipline, and pressure most people would crumble under, Alex is becoming more.

I've seen him laugh when no one's watching. Carry the weight for someone else, work to ease the burden. That's the part no one sees. They just call him the First.

But I see the man underneath. The big brother, the relentless trainer of Tier Ones. The serious one in any setting, a natural leader in the classroom and boardroom. He doesn't think twice about helping, asking how others are doing, and noticing when others need help, even if they refuse to ask. He cares deeply about everyone, about the success of all Wights and the Elitus program.

Alex is one of only four Generation Ones remaining, the first successful group for Elitus. He is ascending into something none of us has touched yet—power, legitimacy, adulthood; the kind Elitus recognizes.

Alex may be stepping into power while I'm just trying not to drown in it.

The rules don't change for girls like me. Combat-classified means useful; not respected, not safe, and never free.

I feel stuck. The rules and restrictions that chain me to a version of myself I'm hating. Most days, I feel I am just a name on a mission log, interchangeable. Disposable.

Alex may graduate, but he's not leaving. He'll still be around. Still commanding the space, wrecking me without even trying.

And I can't decide whether that makes it better or worse.

Because my world doesn't stop. Not for him, not for anyone. Missions are assigned, so training and classes will continue. Combat isn't something I enjoy, but my powers require me to do more than most. I manage it; I wish I had another option. But there aren't any. No future outside of missions and labs.

A laugh behind me yanks me out of my spiral. Mason slips into her seat, legs crossed, all sharp smiles and confidence. She immediately kicks the back of Bastian's chair. He turns with that shit-eating grin of his, unbothered and annoyingly hot in a bad-decision kind of way.

"Ready to party?" Bastian asks, voice low and full of trouble.

Mason smirks. "Are you going to cry when I drink you under the table again, Bastard?" She says, using his nickname. Bastian and Mason are the highest Tier Twos we have. Mental players. They are friends, and Bastian is one of the few guys we allow into our party circle regularly, much to my brother's dismay.

"Not on your life, babe." He winks at her, stretching out in his seat, like he owns the damn world.

Charley, Mason's partner in crime and our resident Firestarter, leans forward and kicks Bastian's chair too, harder this time.

"Who's shielding tonight?" she demands. "Because for a potential X2, you suck."

Even though tonight's party is technically semi-sanctioned, we still have to dodge adult supervision. Especially the kind that reports directly to McGuire.

Bastian jerks his chin toward Jasper, who's tucked into a corner, eyes distant.

"Ames is on it. He's testing some new field dampeners." The dampeners block power surges when things get out of hand. Which they always do.

Mason hums her approval. "Good. The last thing we need is another lecture. Or worse—another lockdown."

Their noise barely registers. My mind's already gone back to him. Alex is sitting on stage, so still, so composed; it should be illegal. His shoulders are square, and his posture is immaculate.

He turns his head, and our eyes lock; just for a second, one breath, one pulse. But it's enough to make my heart stutter and the air catch in my throat. The pull between us, the one that I can always feel beneath the surface, tightens.

His gaze is unreadable, calm, collected, and distant.

Then he looks away.

Alex Clarke doesn't break the rules.

But tonight? I'll make him want to.

Two

Alex

I've stood in this hall before. For lectures, events, meetings. But tonight, it feels like a countdown. As Elitus takes the stage and sits, the air in the grand hall shifts. It thickens, not just with expectation, but with weight. A sense of finality. The kind that settles into your spine.

Recognition has never been Elitus' style. Commendations come behind closed doors, not banners and ceremony. Even the Winter Ball, the biggest event on the calendar, wasn't about legacy; it was about optics.

Controlled celebration, scripted comfort. All to showcase the power of Elitus. The control they have.

But this? This is different. And it feels personal.

With only four of us left in Generation One, the gravity of the moment is impossible to ignore. We are no longer students or trainees. We are the blueprint—the first proof of concept. Everything they've built since it started with us.

Now, we have become the face of the future.

Everything is intentional. Every banner that ripples from the rafters, deep violet with black and silver embroidery, regal and severe. Every beam of light, the overhead chandeliers that cast a pale, surreal glow that reflect off the polished stone and surgical steel. Even the Elitus Board, seated in their arc of authority, looks sculpted for the event.

Elitus has always operated without oversight. A single board, unchanged since the split twenty years ago, decides everything: missions, housing, training, even how we're allowed to interact. It's not just about discipline. It's about risk mitigation. About control.

We're not students or trainees; we're assets. Enhanced, dangerous weapons they keep pointed in the right direction, with just enough comfort to keep us compliant.

I clench my hands at my side. My pulse unsteady. There's pride and fear. I trained for this; we all did. But no one trained us for what comes next. For being more than an experiment. For what it means to be a leader. I just hope that I can help change things, change the way Elitus operates.

Because it's restricting us, limiting us. It's disengaging, and for the younger Gens, it's becoming an issue. One Elitus is ignoring.

But as I sit here, as the speeches begin, for once, I don't just hear the words; I feel them. And it motivates me even more.

When Pepe, Dr. Mason to the outside world, steps onto stage, it steadies something in me. In all of us. He knows how to speak to a crowd without pandering.

"The Elitus welcomes all family, friends, and members of our program here tonight to recognize our Generation One graduates — the first to complete the full academy training and evaluations. When this program started over thirty years ago, the goal was simple: to enhance the impossible. Advance our military. Push the limits of science and evolution. Agent X wasn't the result we expected, but it became a success we couldn't ignore. These Wights—our children—are not just gifted. They are proof. Of adaptation. Of resilience. Of what happens when limits are replaced with legacy."

Where Pepe's words cut deep, Dr. Ross, Kyle's father's voice, carries like water; gentler, but no less deliberate.

"What you see before you isn't just the result of science. It's a sacrifice. Every advancement we've made, every breakthrough in the combat systems, genetics, cognitive expansion, and field response, is because of them. Generation One was our hypothesis. Generation Two and Beyond is proof. We are no longer chasing potential. We are shaping the future."

Then comes Dr. Miller, soft smile in place, but all clinical precision. He buries any pride in our success beneath the efficiency of his words.

"Our Tier One candidates manipulate elements: fire, water, air, plasma, metal. Tier Two are masters of telekinesis, healing, and mental combat. Tier Threes ... well, we still don't fully understand what they're capable of, but it exceeds any pre-conceived notions."

"These students didn't just adapt to their powers; they shaped them. Refined them, helped us rewrite what we thought was biologically possible. This ceremony is more than a marker. It's a declaration."

Applause fades as the families shift in their chairs. Then he stands.

Dr. Robert Clarke. My father. The room locks into silence.

Impeccable as ever. Tailored, composed, and unreadable, he doesn't need theatrics. His presence demands respect. "Tonight, we recognize those who have completed the Elitus program. You are no longer students; you are the leaders."

"Your names are known. Your training is complete. From this day forward, you are not just operatives. You are mentors. Instructors. Role Models. The future. Your designation medals are more than symbols. They are your responsibilities. Wear them accordingly."

His gaze holds mine; one breath, one warning, one passing of the torch.

Then the words come, crisp and final, as my name is called.

"Alexander Robert Clarke. Generation One. High One."

My name echoes across the hall. I rise, adjust my collar and breathe. I feel a slight shield cover come down around me, stabilizing me. I recognize the signature. Mason. She always takes care of her family and friends.

Shields are Wight's first defense against outside threats; invasive powers, even our own volatile emotions. As energy levels fluctuate, the ability to raise a shield or drop one over another becomes essential, not just for protection but for strategic control.

But the most vital function of shielding isn't physical. It's emotional. Shields keep others out of your head, your thoughts, your fears, and the things you don't want anyone to see.

Mason and Bastian mastered it first. They didn't simply perfect shielding; they defined it. Teaching the rest of us how to protect not only our minds, but our sanity. Now, shielding isn't just a skill. It's survival. And it's woven into every part of our daily life.

I cross the stage, my steps echoing louder than they should. A hundred eyes burn into my back. Then he's there—my father, steady as a stone.

He drapes the platinum and black medallion over my neck. Tier One, Level Three, referred to as a High One. It feels heavier than I expected: a target and a crown.

He clasps my shoulder, firm and brief. Not emotionless—but efficient. A gesture that means more because it comes without words.

I nod once.

Descending the stairs and moving toward the front row, I catch my mother's gaze. Joanne's smile is radiant—soft in a way that loosens the tension around my chest. I nod to her, and she presses her hand to her heart.

I exhale. Just once. Then Kyle's name slices through the silence.

"Kyle John Ross. Generation One. X Three."

X. Off-scale. Beyond classification.

Kyle doesn't just possess Tier Three power; he's redefined it. He broke through all the levels and set a new standard for them. That, plus his cocky attitude that never wavers, is the reason they call him the King.

His walk is confident, in a custom-tailored suit, which highlights his lean swimmer's body. Kyle is all about speed and precision. He doesn't need to hit the gym to excess as I do. His auburn hair is styled into a modern, slightly tousled quaff. He looks like the playboy he is. But tonight, there's a flicker of restraint in his jaw. A weight behind his eyes. His father places his medallion over his neck and pulls him into an embrace—quick, but real.

Kyle slides into the seat beside me, looking down at the medallion around his neck. "Told you I'd make history," he mutters.

"You always do," I say, and we bump shoulders, quiet, familiar. Kyle and I are both natural leaders, though on different battlefields. I am more of a leader here at the academy and in the labs. Kyle leads on the field. Currently, the strongest power in our ranks, and the relentless trainer for all Tier Threes.

"Wyatt Nathaniel August. Generation One. X One."

Wyatt's powers are elemental; he has mastered all of Tier One. But that's never really been his story. It's his mind. His ability to synthesize intel and strategies is faster than any AI prototype Elitus assessed, a certified genius. He's known as The Teacher.

Wyatt looks the part, usually in a sweater vest he takes endless shit for, or preppy attire, but he has never cared what anyone thinks. He is brilliant, supportive, and a huge part of the academy's success.

His father claps as Wyatt crosses the stage, but it's Dr. Katherine Ames who gives him his medal. After it's placed, she smiles and whispers, "Congrats." He hugs her, and whispers back to her, "Thanks, Mom."

Kyle and I both smile as her composure cracks. Not his biological mom, but the one that helped raise him and took him under her wing when his mother ignored him. Dr. Ames has tears when they separate. She takes a deep breath and tries to compose herself.

The crowd softens, emotions spilling over.

Then it's Wyatt's best friend and Dr. Ames' daughter's turn.

"Katelyn Ann Ames. Generation One. High One."

If Kyle's the King, then Kate is the Queen. She is the eldest female Wight. She is also my counterpart in being the face of Gen One and Elitus. We are both controlled, methodical perfectionists bound by the rules and responsibilities of leadership and legacy.

Kate is beautiful and elegant, with long, slim lines, and is usually in a power skirt and business suit. Today she is wearing something a little softer, but no less powerful. She wears a deep emerald dress that clings to her curves and shows just enough leg to drag every male's eyes down them to her ice pick heels. At 5'10" Kate is the tallest girl on campus, and she stands above most, especially since she doesn't step out of the dorms unless she is wearing three-inch heels. She walks the stage, as if she is on the runway, with a soft smile on her face as she gets her medal from her mother.

Dr. Ames embraces her tightly, and they whisper back and forth, which makes them both smile.

The weight of the moment softens around us, a celebration of sorts.

But not for long. Dr. Ross steps up again to close out the ceremony. "To the first generation of Elitus Wights: may your future reflect your legacy. And may those who follow, exceed even your greatest accomplishments."

I've never liked the attention. But tonight, it wraps around me like armor. The applause rises, a storm breaking.

Families stand, and people move. The tension breaks into conversations, into pride, into smiles and hugs.

Mason is the first to reach me—sharp elbows, quick stride, mischief not contained. "Look at you. You looked so confident up there," she teases, reaching up to flick my medal. "Ready to lead the masses?"

I smile. "I may be their leader here, but not in the field. That goes to the X."

I nod toward Kyle Ross, ever the performer, basking in the attention of his family, including his sister, the striking redhead in a bold green dress standing beside him, Mason's roommate and best friend, Charley.

Mason catches my expression and smirks. "That's only because Kyle kisses McGuire's ass," she jokes, her tone light. McGuire heads the military side of Elitus and Mason's archenemy most days.

"You going to salute me or hug me?" I ask, lifting an eyebrow.

She rolls her eyes and wraps her arms around me. "I'm proud of you, Alex. Really."

I squeeze her back. "I couldn't have done any of this without you."

"Damn right you couldn't," she says, laughing before she squeezes me one more time before heading off to congratulate the rest.

The ceremony is over, but my mind's already working. I continue to take in the rest of the crowd: the military arm, McGuire, Thompson, and Stephen Moore collaborating near the back. The science arm: my father, Dr. Miller, Dr. Ross, and Dr. Ames, faces full of smiles at the refreshment table with their spouses.

I observe the room for a minute before heading toward my family.

The room is alive, friends chatting, parents laughing too loudly; like they don't sense the undercurrent.

It's there beneath the polished floor, the pride, the applause, something simmers.

This wasn't just an ending.

It was a call to arms.

A shift in the world we were born into.

And I'm not on the sidelines anymore.

I'm at the front of it.

This moment marked the end of something. But more than that, it feels like the beginning; of responsibility, of danger, of a war we haven't named yet. And I'm no longer watching it unfold. I'm leading it.

Legacy clings, a second skin on me. But as we peel away from the crowd, the night takes on a different beat.

I leave the Escalade behind at our parents' and drive something that feels more like me. The vintage BMW my father gave me for my twentieth birthday. Sleek, low to the ground, built for control. It's exactly what I need tonight.

I drive Mason, Mya, and Max back to the dorms. The music hits us before the building does, shaking the air like a heartbeat that's too loud to ignore. The party's already in full swing.

RJ stayed home—he always does. He still lives at home by choice. Aimee? She's stuck with Mom, fuming. That's the price she pays for not being in combat.

Our so-called babysitters are off duty, which means the rules are about to be forgotten.

Mason grins as she hops out of the car, stretching like she has been locked up for years. "God, I missed this place."

"One week at home with our parents is a violation of human rights," I mutter.

"Aimee sure thinks so. She's already planning to join next time."

The front doors swing open, and cheers erupt inside as Mason's already halfway through the door, a queen returning to her kingdom.

Max smirks. "They missed her."

"Someone has to keep up with Charley," I reply. We head to the door, but I stop short, falter as something changes, the air bends slightly, my gut tightens without cause, then I feel it. That spark, the buzz under my skin, the one that only ever comes from her.

And there she is. The magnet I can't ignore for the life of me.

Andy hits me like a hurricane, warm arms around my neck, laughter in my ear, glittering eyes, inches from mine.

"Hi," I manage, catching her instinctively, steadying both of us.

"Hey, handsome," she purrs, slurring just enough to make my stomach twist.

She's radiant, wild and flushed. Her blond hair falls in loose, messy waves, her skin glowing, lips glossy with something I want to taste but won't, can't.

Her fingers slide down my chest, teasing the edge of the medallion around my neck. "You clean up nice, Clarke," she says, and all I want to do is take a step closer and close the gap between us.

But her power's bleeding through, buzzing against my shields, testing them. She's always too close to my edges. "Andy," I say low, a warning she won't hear. "You're smashed."

"So?" Her voice makes my body tighten. She's playing, daring me.

She rises onto her toes, leaning in—I pull back and the moment breaks.

I see it, just a flicker, a fracture in her smile. And then she's laughing it off, spinning it like I imagined a crack in her armor. "Alex, are you blushing?"

I let go of her arms. "Maybe, but that's not the point."

She shrugs, as if I didn't just dodge a bullet. "You're no fun," she whispers, then grabs my hand and pulls me inside.

I try to steady myself. To shift back into the room, but the chaos doesn't wait. Lights, music, bodies in motion, voices rising over the pulse of bass-heavy beats. It's wild, loud, and alive. A jungle built from our kind, and Andy thrives in it.

This place wasn't made for comfort; it was built for containment. The dorms are home to all the combat-enabled Wights, the majority of which are Gen Ones, Twos, and Threes. Our siblings, Mya and RJ, are the only Gen Fours that are tough enough to earn a space here, but only Mya stays at the dorms. At capacity, thirty-two live across four floors, each with suite-style rooms and bare-bones kitchenettes. There's a shared common area with a full kitchen, couches that are never clean, and a basement with a gym, a study zone, and a library most of us pretend to use.

Out back, there's a wraparound deck, an in-ground pool, and basketball courts that rarely see actual games. It looks like freedom. Sometimes it feels like it. But more often, it's just a gilded cage—one of the few spaces we're allowed besides the training center or home.

Tonight, the place is overflowing. The common area spills onto the porch; the sliding doors are open, allowing the sound, sweat, and energy to pulse into the night. The bar in the back, built unofficially by Mason and Bastian a few years ago, has become the center of gravity. No one stopped them. Most of us need alcohol.

Especially the Tier Twos.

Mental noise is a bitch, emotions, thoughts, static bleeding in through even the best shields. Alcohol dulls the edges. Not entirely, but enough. And with how our Wight metabolism and self-healing operates, it takes more than a few drinks to feel anything. A heavy hand is the only way to stay even remotely buzzed.

Andy weaves us through the crowd—her leading, me trailing, always half a step behind where I want to be. Now and then, she glances back, her grin daring me to close the space.

She's stunning, every bit of her. Petite, but with curves that test every ounce of my self-control. But beneath the flirty smirk and perfect bone structure is a fighter. Andy isn't just another pretty girl lost in the party crowd; she's a weapon.

Already testing in the High Threes, her name's coming up more often in mission briefs. She's getting deployed more. The kind of more that's dangerous, that keeps me up at night.

And it pisses me off. Not because she can't handle herself, but because I can't stand the thought of her walking into a situation without me there to pull her back.

She doesn't slow, doesn't wait. Andy moves as if havoc is hers to command.

We hit the edge of the common room, and the makeshift bar comes into view—string lights casting a dim glow over the bar.

Her twin brother, Roarke, one of my best friends and a long-time suffering bartender, is stacking red cups like he's preparing for war.

Andy leans over the counter, full tilt. She's changed out of her dress, and her jeans leave nothing to the imagination. My jaw tightens as I look away.

Roarke scowls. "Really?"

"Fuck off," she says, sweet as poison, grabbing a bottle of tequila like it's a family heirloom. She pours the shots with practiced ease and lifts hers toward me, eyes gleaming.

"To our leader," she purrs, voice laced with sugar and venom. There's a bite in the way she says it; something sharp and familiar. Personal.

She's poking again; prodding, waiting to see if I'll snap.

"To X," I mutter, knocking it back with her.

She grins around the rim of her glass, then downs a second before I can stop her. Her tongue flicks across her lip, and the heat it sparks in my chest is immediate and unwelcome.

She goes for a third. I catch her wrist—firm, but not rough.

"Slow down, Andy."

The game she is playing flips fast. One second soft, then the next shattered. Her eyes flare, all that playfulness evaporating in an instant. What's left is raw, hurt. She jerks her arm back as if I burned her.

"Fuck you, Alex. You might run the show out there, but in my life? No one tells me what to do."

She's gone, disappearing into the crush of bodies before I respond. Leaving me standing in her wake, her presence still buzzing under my skin.

Roarke's voice pulls me back, already sliding a cup across the counter.

"She's unstoppable at this point," he mutters. "I've tried. Just watch her back, yeah?"

I nod automatically, then catch the shift in his expression. "I don't like the way Connor's looking at her."

My gaze sweeps the room, zeroing in on the far wall. Connor Stevens. Leaning against it, like he owns the place, with his crew of degenerates flanking him. His eyes fixed on Andy and my sisters. And not in a way I like.

Not just watching, but hunting. He is a combat, but a minor player. He lives here at the dorms, but we've never been friendly. A Gen Three like Mason and Charley, he always rubs me the wrong way. Fortunately, I rarely have to interact with him or any of his buddies.

Something ugly and territorial rises in me—fast, sharp, uninvited.

I slam back the scotch Roarke handed me, drop the cup, and grab a beer instead. I need something to hold. Something to keep my hands from curling into fists.

I push through the crowd and head toward the card table, where the actual power is gathered.

Andy's perched on a chair, legs crossed, half-listening to stories and entertaining the table. Mason sits beside her, bottle in hand, eyes sharp despite the alcohol. Across from them, Mya lounges, calm and coiled like always. And Charley's twirling a flame between her fingers, daring someone to piss her off.

They're a force, the four of them, the party girls. They are untouchable, unapologetic, commanding attention without even trying.

Bastian's there too, sprawled out with that ever-present smirk like he's watching the world burn and loving every second. He is their sidekick; needing alcohol as much as Mason does, he is her partner in both training and drinking. He has been a constant in her life since she was an infant, always working together, working through things. The two of them are a big reason Elitus and the Wight program is successful.

I look around the room, getting a pulse for the vibe in the dorms. It's already off the rails.

I head to them and slide into the open chair. Mason groans, "Alex, you can't hang. Go cry in the corner with your honor and your medals."

Charley cackles, clearly a few shots ahead of everyone else.

Andy doesn't look at me. She doesn't have to; I can feel her. Her awareness grazes mine like a fingertip along a fault line.

Mya watches the entire table like she's cataloging it, drinks, glances, tension levels.

Bastian's shuffling the deck like a goddamn magician. His fingers flash and flick the cards into place with casual arrogance.

"Not exactly fair playing cards with a mind reader," I say, glancing between Mason and Bastian. They are both proficient as Tier Twos, mental warriors, and they seem to lean into it tonight.

The game starts. I try to focus; I really do. But Andy is a hell of a distraction, whether on purpose or by accident. She pulls my focus. We play a couple of hands. Most of the conversation is Mason getting updates on what she missed in the last week. She is happy to be back at the dorms, having been able to flee our parents and home. Even though Kennedy and RJ are there, Mason has been independent and in the dorms for almost eight years now. So, being back under mom and dad's roof was a change for her.

However, her joy is cut short, because the second Riddick slides into the seat beside Charley, Mason tenses. Riddick Moore is one of my closest friends. He, Roarke, and I are gym partners and have a level of friendship that I value and consider sacred. But even with that friendship, he doesn't take it easy on any of his peers in training. Even my sister. He's brutal to Mason.

Three seconds, that's all she gives him. Then her expression shuts down, shields wrapping around her like armor, and she walks away.

Mason's still furious with him ever since the last mission. Riddick pushes too hard, too often. Between him and Kyle, she's always on the defensive. She pretends she doesn't care. But I know better.

Charley's smile wavers, watching Mason go. But when Jared, Riddick's identical twin, drops into the empty seat, she shifts, all charm and laughter again, like nothing happened.

I sigh and drag my hand through my hair.

The nights just started.

And the damage? It's already in motion.

THREE

Alex

Time blurs. Riddick and I lean against the bar, half-empty beers in hand, silently watching the room unravel around us.

Then Mason storms through the side doors like a fuse already lit; cheeks flushed, curls wild, a new bottle dangling from one hand like a challenge.

She yells, "Shots!" Already unscrewing the cap and pouring. Her voice is too bright, too sharp. She downs one without blinking, then grabs Ryker by the collar and drags him toward the pool table, her laughter loud and boisterous.

Riddick's jaw ticks beside me, his fingers tightening around the bottle.

"She's out of control," I murmur.

"She gets to be, for one night," Riddick says as he watches her like a man bracing for impact. He wasn't at the last party, the one that got her under house arrest, but I know he heard all about it. "She's tired of carrying the weight of being better. Tonight, she's choosing not to."

Mason is a flash fire I can't contain, but it's not the only one burning tonight.

Across the room, Andy is dancing, laughing, glowing. Her hair spills over her shoulders as she moves in tight with a group of Gen Threes, her body fluid and loose, top riding high as she throws her head back in a full-bodied laugh. Then her eyes flick to mine—slow, deliberate—and the look she gives me burns through the space between us.

It's not just a look; it's a test.

And I'm failing by staying.

I grit my teeth and nod toward the balcony. "Come on," I mutter to Riddick, already pushing through the crowd

The noise cuts off like a slammed door. Out here, the air is cooler. The night is quieter, but no less heavy.

We drop into old Adirondack chairs, the wood creaking beneath us. Weathered from storms, parties, and late-night talks like this one. I toss Riddick a beer, pop the cap off mine, and look at the main campus.

The academy glows in the dark, centered like a target in the quad, surrounded by the sprawl of Elitus: training towers, science wings, offices, glass hallways, and underground tunnels all hiding the reality of the power of Agent X.

"I feel ancient," I mutter, shaking my head. "Andy's blitzed. She does not know what she's doing."

Riddick takes a sip, then side-eyes me. "She knows exactly what she's doing, Alex. She's not the confused one."

I let out a humorless laugh. "Yeah? What am I then—just the idiot who follows rules he doesn't even believe in?"

"No," he says, turning to face me fully. "You're the idiot who is half in love with her and too afraid to admit it."

The words hit harder than they should. I look away, my jaw clenched, my throat dry.

"And what do you suggest I do, huh?" I ask quietly. "Tell my dad to go screw himself? Tell Elitus that their golden boy wants to break protocol and hook up with a girl under his command and a year away from graduating?"

Riddick shrugs. "If that's what you want."

I glare at him. "Or," he adds, "you could stop pretending you're not drawn to her, that you are protecting her by pushing her away. Be honest. Tell her you're not cold because you don't care—you're cold because you care too damn much, and that scares the hell out of you."

I stare at the horizon, jaw tight, and take a sip of the beer in my hand.

"You're seriously giving me relationship advice now?" I mutter. "Since when are you my shrink?"

He smirks. "Since you started looking like you were going to crack when you're near her. And since you seem to be unable to avoid her..."

He's not wrong.

I hate how much he sees. How easily he reads me. Riddick's abilities, like Mason's, stretch across all three tiers. Andy's been baiting me for weeks.

Every smirk. Every casual brush of her fingers across mine doesn't feel casual at all. She's trying to get a reaction. Trying to make me choose, to make me break the rules.

And every time I don't, I lose a little more of her. A little more of myself.

I take another long pull from the bottle, and stare at the sky, letting the silence stretch. "I've spent my whole life trying to be the guy everyone can count on. I follow orders, keep it clean, and set an example for the others. I don't want things for myself. That's not how it works."

Riddick's silent for a beat. "Maybe that's the problem."

I glance at him. He doesn't flinch. "You keep trying to be what everyone expects," he says. "But the minute someone sees you for who you are, like Andy does, you flinch. You think pushing her away is noble? But all it's doing is making her feel disposable."

That one lands like a gut punch. Blowing out a breath, I tilt my head back against the chair and stare at the sky. The stars are only slightly visible tonight, blurred by haze, distance, the sheer weight of what's coming.

I huff out a bitter laugh. "Yeah? Let's talk about you, then." I pause for a beat. "Maybe if you stopped riding Mason like she's a damn recruit; she wouldn't look at you like she's ready to kill you."

He tenses beside me.

"I'm not blind or stupid, Riddick. I've seen the way you look at her. And I've seen how much harder you are on her, the closer she gets to leveling up. You're not pushing her to strengthen her. You're afraid of what happens if you stop."

His silence confirms it.

"I push her," he says slowly. "Because she deserves to be the strongest. Because she's better than they'll ever admit. Then all of us. But, yeah, I also push her because if I don't, I'll forget there's a line altogether."

I sigh; we are in the same boat. It's the same damn story; different names, but the same fears, same refusal to leap, to take the risk

"Guess we're both cowards," I say.

Riddick raises his bottle again. "Cheers to that."

We drink in silence, the cool night thick with everything unsaid.

I feel Mason before I hear her. That specific energy: sharp, loud, impossible to ignore.

The door creaks open. Mason steps out like a thunderclap in heeled boots; arms wide, presence loud, alone this time, no Ryker in tow, thank God.

"Lost your dance partner?" Riddick drawls, lifting a brow without looking at her.

Mason smirks, and I don't miss the glint in her eyes, the one that says she knows exactly how much that question gets under his skin. She enjoys this.

"Yep. And a lot more, they're all crying that they're tired. Babies. Oh—and we're almost out of beer and alcohol."

"Good," I mutter, my tone clipped. "You need to cut off your girls, anyway. They're going to stir up too much drama."

"I love drama," Andy says as she steps outside, voice playful but slurred.

Her steps are rough, too rough, like she is on the verge of something. Roarke is right behind her; I can already see the tension forming like storm clouds in her eyes.

"Dammit, Roarke," she snaps, whirling on her twin. "Go bother someone else. I said I wanted air, so I'm getting air."

Her voice has a bite, but it's the kind that sounds more desperate than angry. She's cracking. Her power's running wild beneath the surface, energy pulsing in waves I can feel. I watch her jaw clench; hands curl into loose fists. She's trying to get control.

But it's not working.

Roarke doesn't answer. He exhales slowly trying to keep calm. He knows what is coming. I do, too.

Andy's power flares, angry and unstable, overriding her control. She can't burn it off or shield it, not with all the alcohol swimming in her veins.

She storms off but stumbles forward, knees buckling as the alcohol finally wins. And I am already moving, catching her before she hits the ground. Her weight slumped against me. She smells of tequila and citrus body spray.

"Jesus, Andy," I breathe, steadying her with one arm around her back and the other beneath her knees, as I lift her up. Her skin burns against mine, electricity coiling up my arms like a live wire. Every instinct I have—combat, control, restraint—is shouting at me to back off. But there's another voice, louder. One that wants to pull her closer, bury my face in her neck. Forget the rules.

Her head rolls against my shoulder, eyes half-lidded, her breath hitting my collarbone. I drop more shields, otherwise, I may do something stupid. Like, kiss her.

"Whoa..." she slurs, blinking slowly. "You smell really good."

"Fantastic," I mutter. I see Roarke's expression tighten, the muscle in his jaw jumping. He's not an idiot, and as one of my best friends, I know I am crossing the line with my thoughts on his twin. It's getting harder and harder not to react to her. "Take her to her room, Alex. I'll be there in a minute."

"No," Andy protests weakly, pushing at my chest, but there's no real fight. "I'm not done yet."

"Yes, you are," I say flatly, adjusting her in my arms as I head toward the balcony doors. Rescuing her again.

"Don't carry me," she mumbles. "Makes it too easy to fall in love with you."

That stops me cold, just for a heartbeat. My grip tightens. But I push through the crowd with Andy in my arms. A few people whistle or call something crude, but I ignore them. All I can focus on is how light she feels, fragile.

Her head lolls again, cheek brushing my neck.

"Do you ever think," she mumbles, "if things were different, we could be together?"

I freeze halfway down the hall. Her words hang in the air like smoke—if things were different.

I want to tell her yes. That I already do.

I have been falling for her since she looked at me like I was more than just the golden boy, Robert's son.

But I don't... I keep walking, every step heavier than the last.

I reach her door. She's half-asleep; limbs heavy, breath slowing, soft murmurs slipping past her lips. I nudge her door open with my foot and carry her inside. The scent of her room hits me like a punch to the chest, citrus and linen and something unmistakably Andy.

I lower her onto the bed as gently as I can. She shifts and murmurs something incoherent, one hand reaching instinctively toward me before falling limp again. I ease the blanket over her, brushing a strand of blond hair off her forehead, swallowing hard, trying not to think about how many times I've done this. How many times have I cared for her in silence, in secret?

I remove her boots, grab a glass of water and aspirin, and set them on the nightstand. It's the only way I'm allowed to care for her—behind closed doors, in moments she won't remember when no one is watching.

I should leave. But I don't. Not right away.

Her face is peaceful now, stripped of the fire and armor she wears like a second skin. I feel her pull like gravity, invisible but relentless. There's something beneath her surface that never stops humming. Something wild that's matching the noise in me.

However, the future waiting for us? It's not built for softness. Not for moments like this.

The Elitus project is evolving. Missions are increasing, and the stakes are higher than ever before. Now that I have graduated, I plan on taking a more active role. I will steer the program from the inside—alongside Kate, Kyle, and Wyatt. To fix the machine before it chews more of us up.

To do that, I must stay clean. Controlled. Untouchable. Even when I feel like I'm coming apart from the inside out.

Not because I'm trying to be the golden boy.

But because I can make it better. For the next ones, for Mya, for Kennedy, for kids who don't have a choice. For people like Andy.

She hates the pressure; hates the way combat strips us bare. But she still suits up and walks into the line of fire. Not because she wants to—but because no one gave her another way out.

She's not wild for the thrill, but because it's the only way she still feels in control.

The door creaks behind me. Roarke steps inside, his expression tight but thankful. He meets my eyes and nods once. I nod back. No words needed. This part of the job, the part where we try to keep her safe, that's something we both understand.

I slip past him, back into the hallway.

The door clicks shut behind me.

And I walk away.

But in the back of my mind, one thought sticks like a blade I can't pull loose. How many more times can I do this? Before I'm unable to walk away.

Andy

I wake up too clear-headed for someone who tried to drink herself into oblivion, Wight resilience and self-healing at its finest.

No pounding headache. No nausea. Just a dry throat and a familiar, gnawing weight in my chest. Regret. Shame. Something between the two. I stare at the ceiling; the sunlight slicing through the blinds like judgment. It's too bright, too clean. Like the day is mocking me for surviving another round of my self-destruction.

I sit up slowly, bracing myself for the dizziness that never comes. I didn't drink enough to forget everything—just enough to be reckless. To feel brave. Or numb.

My clothes are wrinkled; someone took my boots off and pulled a blanket over me. A water bottle and aspirin are waiting at the nightstand, little trophies to commemorate the mess. I don't need to ask who left them.

I already know, Alex.

He is always the protector, the savior, the one to fix what's broken and leave before it turns into something real.

I press a hand to my chest, half-expecting it to ache the way it did when he walked away. But it's not the pain I feel. It's the absence of it. Like I've gone numb in all the places that used to burn.

Why do I keep doing this to myself?

Every time I get close to him, I push harder. Flirt more. Drink deeper. Like I'm trying to shake something loose in him that refuses to move. But it never works. He doesn't flinch, doesn't bend, doesn't break.

Alex Clarke doesn't take risks. Not the kind that matters.

I swing my legs over the edge of the bed. Inside me? It's a mess. And the worst part is I remember it all. The way I leaned into him, how I touched his jaw. I tried with every ounce of me to make him see me. Not Roarke's sister, not a walking disaster. Just me.

Even so, he stepped back.

Still, he left.

I take the aspirin and water, not because I need them, but because it gives my hands something to do. Something that doesn't feel like I am falling apart.

There's a knock at the door. My stomach flips for a second. I let myself believe.

Then I hear Roarke's voice.

"Andy?"

"I'm up," I say, keeping my voice steady.

He steps inside, a coffee in one hand and quiet disappointment in the other. But he doesn't scold me. He doesn't press. He sets the cup on my dresser and leans against the wall, arms crossed.

"You look... annoyingly fine," he says.

"Sorry to ruin the drama."

I try to smirk, but it slips before it lands. Roarke watches me like he's measuring how deep the damage goes.

"You remember everything?"

Alex's arms around me. The sound of his voice when he thought I wouldn't remember. The way he didn't kiss me, even when I begged him with my eyes. "Too much."

Roarke nods slowly, then says what we're both thinking.

"You were reckless last night."

I laugh, dry and bitter. "That's not exactly news."

"No," he agrees. "But it's getting worse."

And that's the problem, the part I can't deny. It is getting worse. I drink not to party, but to feel normal. To drown out the noise, the expectations, my self-doubt. Liquid courage.

I never asked for these expectations, this power. I've spent years being too loud, too wild, too much, and still not enough.

Not for my father. Not for Elitus. Not for Alex.

Alex still sees a girl who can't be trusted with her choices. Someone wild and out of control. Not the woman standing in front of him, asking to be seen, to be loved.

Roarke pushes off the wall. "You're going to have to talk to him, eventually."

"Talk to him?" I scoff. "About what?"

He pauses in the doorway, his expression unreadable. "About how you keep setting yourself on fire just to see if he'll burn with you."

Then he leaves, and I sit there. Singed from the inside out. And I hate to admit that maybe he is right, and the worst part is I don't know how to stop it.

FOUR

Andy

After the last party, I attempt to stay away from alcohol.

It's not a huge declaration. I didn't announce it or make a big deal. I quietly started skipping the drinks, slipping water into red cups. It's easier that way. Mason is also on the same page for once, both of us low on tolerance for drama and high on unspoken things neither of us is ready to unpack.

We are on Mason's couch, surrounded by junk food, wrapped in old blankets, and halfway through the worst '80s rom-com known to humankind. Popcorn litters the floor. The smell of sweet candy and greasy pizza hangs heavy in the air. Mason is curled beside me, already scrolling through her phone, looking for what to force us to watch next. Charley sprawls across the beanbag with a bowl of popcorn and M&M's.

It should feel normal, comfortable. And mostly, it does.

But there's still a tension inside me that never goes away.

"What's up with you and Alex?" Marty, a fellow Gen Two combat female and Charley's older sister, asks from the floor, completely unbothered, like she's asking what time it is. I nearly choke on my Diet Coke.

Mason doesn't even try to hide her smirk. She doesn't look up from her phone, but I can feel the 'I told you so' vibrating off her.

"Nothing," I say too quickly, too brightly. My face flushes hot, and I sink deeper into the blanket, wishing I could rewind ten seconds and erase how I panicked.

Marty raises an eyebrow. "Uh-huh."

Even though it's been weeks since that night—since I completely humiliated myself in front of him—Alex has been... around. We can't ever seem to avoid each other.

Not directly. We talk a little, a quick "hey" in the hallway, a nod across the mess hall, polite words passing.

But I feel him.

Every time I walk into a room, I feel his gaze tracking me. Not in a creepy, possessive way, but in that calm, watchful way that makes my skin tingle and my heartbeat stumble.

He's still trying to keep an eye on me. Or just watching over Roarke's twin sister. Because that's all I am, right? Roarke's twin sister.

The girl who nearly kissed him when she was drunk off her ass and said something she shouldn't have. I chew on my straw, avoiding everyone's eyes.

Roarke's been practically glued to my side lately. I turned twenty and expected him to ease up, maybe even treat me like an adult. Instead, every time I so much as breathe near some guy, he's there, looming in the background like some overprotective warden. I get it. I do. But sometimes, it feels like no one sees me for me.

I glance at Mason; I know she wouldn't betray my confidence. But the way she looks at me sometimes, I wonder if she sees more than I want; like she's waiting for me to stop pretending.

The truth? I've had a crush on Alex Clarke since I was fourteen. He was tall, serious, and brilliant in a way that made everyone listen when he spoke. Back then, he rarely looked at me. Just another one of Mason's friends, a female combat, tagging along behind the other Wights.

But lately, it's different. The way he looks at me now, it's not just polite. It lingers; it aches. I can throw a punch, talk back to instructors, and hold my own on missions with guys twice my size. But get me within five feet of Alex, and I'm suddenly unsure of every word that comes out of my mouth.

It's infuriating. Because I know he feels it too. The air shifts when we're close. My whole body reacts. I'm not the only one. I've caught the way his eyes darken when I laugh, the way his hands twitch like he wants to touch me but doesn't. I think that's the main reason he has avoided me. And I hate it because I miss it. I miss him.

"Seriously though," Marty says, poking at a candy wrapper with her toe. "Something is going on. You light up like a Christmas tree anytime he's within ten feet."

"I do not," I grumble, though I know it's true.

Charley lifts her head. "You kind of do. It's adorable. Painful. But adorable."

Mason chuckles. "He does it too. Just... in reverse. Like a Christmas tree with a short circuit. Blinks a little too long."

"Okay, we're done now," I say, hurling a pillow at her. They all laugh, and I force a smile, but inside, the ache curls tighter.

Needing to steer the conversation far, far away from my humiliation, I pivot. "So... how was your mission with Riddick yesterday?" I ask, shooting Mason a grin as I watch her expression twist into immediate scowling mode.

"Jackass Number One and Jackass Number Two joined me," she grumbles, dropping her phone and tearing open a bag of M&M's. Chocolate is her go-to default when she is frustrated.

Jackass Number One: Riddick. Jackass Number Two: Kyle.

"They both acted like they were in charge," Mason continues, her voice rising with indignation, "like I was just there for decoration. As if I haven't been pulling rank on these missions for years."

Mason thrives in combat. She always has. She and Charley were born for action: tough, relentless, and sharp as hell. They fight just as hard as any guy, maybe harder. Especially since, being women in a system that still leans on hierarchy and old assumptions, they've had to prove it every step of the way. But that's the Elitus way.

We were born into it—Wights by birth, by blood, by mandate. But there was never an actual choice. Once our abilities emerged. We were assigned. Evaluated. Trained and tested.

And once you test into combat? That's it; your path is sealed.

I tested Tier Three. Decent teleportation and minor object manipulation. Not enough to light the world on fire; but enough to get on mission rosters.

Roarke and I share the same teleporting ability. The only difference is he's stronger, faster, and a High Tier Three. His offensive capabilities stretch wider. He hits harder. He hates fighting more than I do. But he goes every time. Because if he's there, I won't have to be.

He doesn't say it. Doesn't have to. I see it in every assignment he volunteers for. Every time, he steps in before I can. He carries the burden for both of us—and I love him for it. But it also makes me feel like a liability. Maybe I am the girl who needs watching. Managing.

"Why didn't Roarke go with you?" Marty asks, dragging me back to the moment.

"He was escorting Bastian and Kate on an intel run," Mason says, barely hiding her smirk. All of us glance at each other. Then, we burst out laughing. Poor Roarke.

Bastian and Kate are... a lot. Oil and water. Fire and ice. Bastian's a cocky hothead, explosive and unapologetic. Kate's a composed perfectionist; cool, elegant, and able to ignore everyone's bullshit.

Unless that bullshit is Bastian's.

Let's be real, it always is.

From the outside, Kate seems like a polished beauty queen. But I know better. She's one of the most loyal, driven people I've ever met. A High One, mentally elite, with a mind like a blade, and she's constantly fighting for space in a Gen One team full of powerhouses. She never trips over her words and doesn't second-guess whether she belongs in the room.

And that's no easy feat, especially with Wyatt, Kyle, and Alex—each of them commanding in their own way. It's difficult standing shoulder-to-shoulder with legends when no one gives you a break.

And she does it with heels on. I wish I had her confidence. That calm, collected edge. The way she holds her place with no need to shout to be seen.

Since Gen One graduated two months ago, the entire structure of the academy has shifted. Kate and Alex moved into positions within Elitus HQ; Kyle and Wyatt took on training roles. They're still around, but now they're doing something else. Something official.

They're the future. The leaders.

Elitus Academy has been our world since we were kids, ages seven to twenty, full curriculum wrapped in combat drills, strategy, and endurance training. A boot camp disguised as a school. Most Wight kids still live at home, but not us. Not combat-classified.

We've lived in the dorms on campus for years, since our tenth birthday; that is when the real training begins. We train, serve, run missions. But we don't ask questions.

Not unless we want the answers to hurt.

With the movie Mason picked winding down to its third predictably boring act, she nudges me. "Hey, can you drop off that folder at Wyatt's? It's got teaching assignments in it."

"Sure," I get up, stretching. My legs are asleep, and my brain is restless.

I climb the stairs that lead to the top floor, the Gen One wing. It still feels off-limits, even now. Even though we're adults. Even though I've trained alongside them. There's a weight to the space, like history still clings to the air, whispering that I don't quite belong.

I head toward Wyatt's room, folder in hand, but pause as I pass another doorway.

Alex's door is open.

And... I can't help myself. I stop, lean against the door frame, and watch him.

He's lounging back against his pillows, papers, and folders spread across his lap like he's been there for hours. Dressed in loose sweatpants and a white T-shirt, with his blond hair still damp, fresh from the gym. He lives in the gym and in my head. Roarke, Riddick, and Alex treat that place like a second home.

Alex isn't just a High One. He is dangerous. As Tier Threes, Roarke and Riddick rely on power to amplify their physical strength. Alex doesn't need to. He carves himself into a weapon every single day. Through reps, sweat, practice, and control.

That's who he is. Precision and pressure in a perfect, infuriating package.

My eyes linger too long. He looks up at the soft knock I give; the sound barely echoes off the frame. His gaze finds mine.

And for a second, just a flicker, I see it. That same flicker I keep pretending I imagined. It's not annoyance nor exasperation, but desire.

It flashes behind his eyes like lightning across the water, quick and sharp, gone, before I can be sure. But I swear I felt it. And it leaves me breathless.

Alex

I'm deep in strategy reports—projected deployment shifts for the next quarter, rotation gaps in Tier Two field units, and revisions for the next Gen Four trials. After spending a couple of hours at the gym, I'm trying to finish up the workload. I have been at it for days, the weight of leadership dull and familiar on my shoulders.

The door is open, not because I expected anyone to stop by but because sometimes the silence feels like too much. I don't hear her approach; I don't realize she's there until I feel her. Then I look up. Andy's leaning against the frame, arms folded, loose strands of hair falling around her face, her mouth curled at the corners like she caught me doing something embarrassing.

My brain stutters. I school my expression. But it's too late. Because when our eyes meet, I know she sees it. The unspoken thing I've tried hard to bury.

Why does she always look like this? Like a wildflower begging to be picked. An unwise decision I know better than to want, but do, anyway.

Andy Parrish has been under my skin since she stopped being "Roarke's twin sister" and became her—the girl with the loud laugh, the bright eyes, the impossible energy that burns through every room she walks into. She's chaos, impulse, intensity, and everything I've spent my life training myself not to want.

And yet. She's always there, pushing the line. She teases at the edge of my sanity. Not just in how she acts, but in how she looks at me.

Even now, standing in my doorway like this moment is nothing; she's wrecking me.

I clear my throat and sit up straighter, trying to bring myself back to neutral. She makes me forget everything I'm supposed to be. "Need something?"

I should be aggravated that she's here. That she walked into my space uninvited, that she caught me off-guard with half a mission draft open in my lap and no armor between us. But I'm not. God help me, I'm not. And that probably makes me selfish, but seeing her is always the highlight of my day. My schedule doesn't leave room for much, least of all distractions. And yet, she's the one thing I can't seem to push aside.

But the truth? None of those excuses hold anymore. I'm attracted to her. In ways that run so much deeper than just physical. Though that part? Yes. That's undeniable.

She's beautiful and wild, but it's more than that. It's her fire. Her refusal to be tamed. The way she walks into every room, daring the world to challenge her. The fact is, she goes head-to-head with the other Threes. She demands to stay in combat, even though I know she hates it.

She's unpredictable in ways that should send me running. But I keep coming back. If it weren't for the obligations—combat briefings, the damn law degree—I might've already tried to build something real.

But right now? I don't see how.

So, I keep my distance. Tell myself it's the right thing to do. But then she steps into a room, and every ounce of that logic shatters like glass. Like now. She's in leggings and a hoodie that's not hers, probably Roarke's, draped off one shoulder, exposing just enough collarbone to distract me. Looking comfortable and casual, she looks like she belongs here. She doesn't even realize what she's doing to me.

My attention fractures instantly. She settles on a corner of my bed, barely grazing the papers near my knee, her presence disrupting every thread of focus I've worked so hard to tie together.

She doesn't say much at first, just takes in the chaos of my desk, the papers, the scribbled notes. Her hair falls forward as she leans over, and I have to look away before I do something stupid, like reach out to brush it behind her ear.

No matter how hard I try to deny it, she owns every errant thought in my head. Every part of me that's still young enough to want something just for the sake of wanting it, she stirs that part to life. And that's what terrifies me more than any mission briefing ever could. She shifts closer, brushing the edge of a document.

"Anything interesting?" She asks, voice light but curious.

"Not really. Mostly contracts. Legal stuff."

She nods, but I can feel her watching me. That look. The one that makes me feel like she's reading past the layers. As if she knows something I won't say out loud.

"No parties tonight?" I ask.

"Nope. Junk food and movies in Mason and Charley's room. Mason sent me to drop this off at Wyatt's," she says, holding up a file.

I close a few folders, stacking them neatly, trying to keep my hands busy.

She watches me. And I like that she does.

"Most of the guys went out, I think," I offer casually.

Her smirk is automatic. She tilts her head, reading between the lines like she always does. I don't know whether she thinks it's an invitation. I don't even know if I think it's an invitation.

"Are you headed to bed?" I ask. My voice is quieter than I intended.

She shrugs. "I was... unless you have another suggestion?"

That smile. That half-dare in her tone. It knocks the breath out of me.

I chuckle, forced, almost nervous, but my brain is already thinking. If we were normal, if this were a normal life, I'd take her out for dessert. Or coffee. Or anything that didn't come with a risk assessment attached to it.

But this isn't normal; we don't get that.

We don't get dinner dates and public affection. We get rules, protocols, closed doors and tightrope walks. And yet...

She can port. But as a female Wight, she needs an escort. Technically, I could be her escort.

Don't get me wrong, I've heard stories. I know she and Mason have snuck off base more than once and didn't get caught.

It's not exactly sanctioned, but Elitus turns a blind eye to the guys. It's been happening since we were field-ready and full combat-enabled. For me, that was about five years ago, when our missions increased. A little freedom felt like an earned reward.

But the girls? They're still caged tighter. Mason hates it. That's why she acts out, why she throws parties. Drinks. Rebels. She needs an outlet; they all do.

I know things must change. I'm hoping, between my legal work and Kate's administrative role, we'll push the system into something better. Something more humane, with a purpose beyond being weapons and science experiments. Something to look forward to, a future for all of us. One day I'll change the system, but right now? I just want to forget it exists.

But she's standing here. And everything else, the system, the rules, the future, doesn't seem to matter at this moment. I know this is the part where I'm supposed to walk her to her room and play it safe. But I don't move. Can't, not when every part of me is begging for a second more. For something more, something real, something for me.

It's dangerous. It's impulsive. But for once, I want to want something for myself. Before I lose my nerve, I ask, "Do you want to do something?"

She arches a brow. "Like what?"

"Are you hungry?" I ask before I can talk myself out of it. "We could grab a burger."

She laughs, a soft, genuine sound that hits low in my chest. "Alex, are you suggesting we break the rules?"

My lips twitch. "Maybe."

She grins wider, stepping just a little closer, fingertips grazing mine. "Then lead the way."

FIVE

Andy

I can't believe we're doing this.

As I slide into the booth across from Alex at the local diner, my heart is racing like I just sparred six rounds. The smell of sizzling burgers, melted cheese, and coffee, strong enough to wake the dead hangs in the air. Classic booths, laminated menus, the low hum of conversation. It's so normal it almost feels surreal.

My smile's ridiculous, wide and impossible to hide. I look like a lunatic, but I don't care. This feels different. Special.

Alex settles across from me, dressed down in jeans and a fitted gray shirt. He doesn't look like the Elitus poster boy. He looks... relaxed. He acts as if he belongs here. Like he belongs to me.

He leans back in the booth, his arm casually draped over the top, and gives me that faint, crooked smirk. The one that makes my insides melt. All sexy and confident, with a dash of charm.

"You act like you never get to go out," he teases, voice low and smooth, like a secret passed across the table.

"I do," I say honestly, fingers running over my menu. "But not like this."

Not with him, not without the walls, the rules, the constant awareness of who is watching, and that every move is monitored.

Not without the weight of judgment, my father's voice in my head. It plays on repeat; you're reckless, weak, a mistake, worthless without Roarke. The same tired refrain. My relationship with my father is strained.

Even though I've been away from home for years, even though he's not here to drag me down anymore, the damage sticks. It rewires you. It makes you question everything that comes your way.

But here, with Alex, I can pretend I'm a girl having dinner with a guy she likes. His smirk fades, and I catch the shift in his eyes; concern, doubt, or possibly regret. Something that tightens my stomach instantly.

I feel the words coming before they even leave my mouth. "Sorry," I murmur, ducking my head. "I didn't mean to ruin the mood."

"Don't be," he breathes, and when I look up, his gaze is steady. "I'm not mad. Just... frustrated. With Elitus. I know it's suffocating. I know you, Mason, the others. You feel like prisoners half the time."

That surprises me more than anything. I've always seen him as part of the machine, but he sees more than I give him credit for. "I'm trying to change some things," he adds, fingers drumming lightly on the table like he's thinking ahead.

I blink. "You're what?"

He shrugs, but his jaw tightens. "I'm finishing up my degree in law and government in December and taking my bar at the end of the year. Once I pass the bar, I'll have more leverage with Elitus' oversight. I'm already helping with contract restructuring."

I stare at him for a second. He means it. He's trying to build something real. "McGuire's never going to let that happen," I say flatly, bitterness slipping out before I can stop it.

His lips twitch into something more serious. "It'll take time. But he's already losing ground. Morale is down. The younger generations—Gen Four and Five? They don't want combat. Most of them shouldn't be combat. We must find other paths. Better ones. I'm hoping we can eventually phase the X program into something... voluntary."

I tilt my head, intrigued. "Like the Latents?"

He pauses. Our eyes collide, and there it is again, that flicker. Uncertainty. Maybe even guilt.

"That's a rumor," he mutters. But his tone doesn't match the words. There's too much tension there. Too much truth. The rumors say they're children of test subjects from the first rounds of Agent X, long before Gen One was born. Potential Wights with Latent X abilities. It's all speculation, but it's been floating around more than ever lately.

"But?" I press.

He exhales slowly. "But maybe it's not. Maybe there's something in the early test subjects, a Latent X gene, which was passed down. Elitus is working to figure out how to use it. If so, it changes everything."

I want to believe him. In this version of Alex, sitting across from me, talking about change, about the future, because it's not just about Elitus. It's about us. About whether there's even a place for someone like me in his world.

Because I know what it is like to live in a cage someone else designed. To be told what you are, what you aren't, and what you will never be. My prison isn't just the system; it's the echo of my father's voice in every doubt I have about myself. And no amount of combat training or Tier Three rankings can silence that.

Alex looks at me like he can feel that.

"What's the point of having these abilities if we don't use them?" I ask, parroting the line we've all heard a thousand times. My voice is dry and brittle.

His expression darkens immediately. "That's the bullshit they feed us to keep us from asking questions," he clips. "They never once stopped to ask who we wanted to be. Just what they needed us to become."

The server appears then; young, barely older than us. We order burgers, fries, sodas, and she's gone as quickly as she came.

I sit back, chewing on his words.

"Is that what you want to be?" I ask quietly. "What they need?"

Alex leans in slightly, eyes locked on mine. "No," he says. "I want to be someone who changes it. For the next generation. For my sisters, for people like you."

The words hang there, heavy between us. Something inside me clenches. I don't know if it's hope or fear, or both. My heart stumbles, and we just look at each other. Something shifts.

This isn't just dinner, not a stolen moment; this is the first time I believe that maybe I'm not too much for someone to choose. Maybe I'm just enough for someone to fight for.

The server swings by with a warm smile, balancing our plates with practiced ease. Alex takes the interruption as a chance to shift gears, letting the heavier conversation settle between us like dust in sunlight.

"So," he says, casually nudging his plate into place, "what do you think about the Winter Ball?"

I blink, surprised by the pivot but grateful for the chance to breathe. "It'll be the usual. Weird formal theme. Too much perfume and glitter. Not enough food. And everyone pretending they don't have crushes on each other."

Alex laughs under his breath, eyes glinting with amusement. "That sounds about right."

"And then," I say, grabbing a fry and waving it like a pointer, "we'll all act surprised when there's an after-party in the dorms that Elitus doesn't know about."

"You don't sound thrilled about the after-party," Alex says, voice low, measured. Watching me a little too closely. I try to brush it off with a shrug, but I can't meet his eyes. He's not wrong.

It's hard to explain, even to myself. I am not stupid. I know I make a mess of things when I drink. But it's also the only time I feel... unburdened. Like I can just be. Be me. Loud, flirty, fun, free.

Because when I'm sober, I hesitate. I second guess. I question every look, every glance, every flicker of possibility. Especially with him. When I can't tell if the tension between us is real, or just wishful thinking.

I know my upbringing, verbal abuse, constant insults, and scrutiny at home has caused my insecurities, but every time something goes right, or should go right, I doubt myself. I hear my father's voice, the one that tells me I'm too much, or not enough. Or that I'm only valuable if I am useful. I don't get to be vulnerable or wanted or even seen.

"Andy," Alex says softly. I look up, caught in my mind. And then he reaches across the table and takes my hand in his. My breath catches as his fingers wrap around mine, warm and steady. All I can do is look at our hands and stare at the contrast. His skin is naturally tanner than mine. But our hands are threading together like they've always meant to find each other.

Then, gently, oh so gently, his other hand lifts my chin. And I forget to breathe when our gazes collide. He looks into my eyes, really looks at me. He sees me. And I see it in his eyes. This is something real, raw.

"I don't like your drinking to excess," he says, voice quiet but firm. "Whatever causes that... just know I'm always here to listen. Sober or drunk." He smiles faintly. "Preferably sober."

I laugh, but it comes out fragile, like I'm balancing on a tightrope and the wind just picked up. And I want to tell him the truth, tell him I don't drink to forget; I drink to be free, to be the version of myself that feels worthy of someone like him.

But sitting here, in the soft glow of lights, wrapped in his focus? I don't need a drink. I gather enough courage, flipping my hand over and slowly intertwining our fingers, locking them in place. His hand is bigger, stronger. But we fit. It feels safe. Right.

"If I promise to be sober," I murmur, looking up at him through my lashes, "can you help the rest get a party?"

His laugh rumbles low in his chest, and without warning, he lifts our joined hands and presses a soft kiss to the back of mine. It's barely a touch. But I feel it everywhere.

"I can try," he says. And I don't breathe for a second. That small kiss, a brush of lips. That was a promise. A crack in the walls he keeps around himself. The armor bent slightly, giving a glimpse of something real.

I smile at him, and for once, I don't worry whether it's too much. Maybe this was meant to happen. We are moving forward.

The server returns with the check, oblivious to the emotional shift hanging between us like a thread we're both terrified to pull. He slides his card into the bill folder without a word. Gentleman to the end.

But when we stand, I go to let go of his hand—and he doesn't let me. His grip tightens, just slightly, his thumb brushing across the back of mine. I glance up, surprised. But he looks at me. Steady. Intentional. He doesn't want the moment to end, either. We step into the night, fingers still intertwined. And for once, I don't question it. I hold on.

Alex

The door swings shut behind us with a hollow thunk, and we step into the dark alley behind the diner. The air is crisp and smells faintly of oil and pavement. Streetlights flicker overhead, casting broken shadows across the cracked concrete.

We head toward the far corner of the alley, a discreet, shielded spot out of street view. It's the perfect place to teleport out. Andy walks beside me, unaware of how tight my entire body is. She's laughing softly under her breath, replaying something from dinner.

Then I feel it—not a sound, not a movement. Just a presence, familiar, but wrong. A shift in energy, subtle, deliberate. One that isn't common.

I stop, pulling back on our joined hands. I move Andy back, just forceful enough that she stumbles into me. I shift forward, placing myself between her and the threat, my hand lightly on her waist, steadying her before she can protest.

Stay still.

I don't say it aloud. I don't have to. The message pulses from me to her in silence, a command cloaked in tension. I feel her pulse jump beneath my fingers. Her body stills. Her breath catches. And for once, she listens.

Neither of us are proficient in mental shields. I'm a weapon, meant to be aggressive and offensive. She's a jumper, a Tier Three porter. She moves and delivers. But stealth? Cloaking? That's not what we trained for.

My eyes scan the shadows, searching for the ripple I felt. A disturbance in the energy. A signature just off enough to be deliberate. I wait.

One breath. Two. A tap against her wrist.

A signal, one meant to tell her if we need to move. Her fingers twitch in mine, acknowledging it. But she doesn't pull away.

I exhale and release her. She turns toward me, brows pulled tight. "It's gone," I whisper, but the warmth from earlier, our laughter, the handholding, the soft kiss to her knuckles—it's gone too. Burned off by instinct, by the threat. And now, all that's left is the weight of what could've happened.

She studies me carefully. "PPG?" her voice, just above a whisper.

PPG, Power Principal Group; children like us, products of the Agent X Serum, but not raised under Elitus. A splinter faction. Trained and dangerous in ways we still don't completely understand. Enemies, technically. I've always suspected McGuire manufac-tured the conflict, more about contracts and control than any real ideological split.

Still. If they're here? That's not good. But I can't tell. I didn't recognize the signature, so it wasn't Elitus, but that doesn't mean they were here for us. The area we went to isn't far from the campus, and it's well known that we are here. Dmitri is notorious for having spies and agents, so the presence could just be a coincidence. Could be...

"I don't know," I mutter, but I hear the edge in my voice. I can't hide it. It's sharp, clipped, and tightly controlled. I'm pissed. At myself, the unknown, the risk to her.

Andy nods, but I see it in her eyes. She's unsettled. Shaken. She hates not knowing what's coming, hates being protected like she's fragile. And I get it, but I won't apologize for keeping her safe.

"Take us back," I say. She reaches for me immediately, with no hesitation now. Her fingers curl around my wrist and in the blink of an eye, the alley dissolves. We land back in my room with a soft thud of displaced air.

But the tension? It doesn't go anywhere. Instead, it wraps around us like a storm we can't outrun; still buzzing in my body, crackling between us. Andy steps back first, rubbing her arms as if she is trying to shake it off. But I don't move. I can't.

I should say something. I should break the silence before it breaks us. But I don't. Not right away. Somewhere between the alley and here, I let the lines blur again. I let myself want her. And now, I'm not sure how to go back to how we were before.

"I'm sorry," I say, my voice low and heavy.

Her head snaps up. "For what, Alex?"

I sigh. God, there is too much packed into the question. I think to myself about a million different ways I could answer it. Sorry for hoping for a future we can't have; sorry for looking at you like we could be something, for giving in to something I shouldn't want. For not knowing how to be the guy you deserve, or how to be strong enough to put you above the demands of Elitus and leadership.

Instead, I go with what I can say: "Sorry for putting you in danger."

She blinks, surprised. Then, she laughs, a genuine laugh. Sharp and unfiltered, echoing off the walls like it doesn't belong in the aftermath of what we just went through.

"You're kidding, right? Jesus, Alex, do you not know the assignments I've been sent on lately?"

My stomach twists. I don't. My jaw clenches. I thought I had access to all the mission logs, especially for those active in the field, but from the look on her face, I question that.

If they've sent her out without proper coverage, I'll gut whoever signed off on it. It makes me wonder what else is being kept from me.

Her tone shifts quickly. She's trying to backtrack and smooth it over. "Alex, trust me, that was nothing. Although I'm glad you were with me," she adds with a grin, bumping her shoulder against mine. "I hear you're pretty badass when you want to be."

I should smile, but I am too focused on the flicker of heat in her eyes. The way she is suddenly so close to me, in my space. I don't move back, although I should. But I don't want to.

"Andy," I murmur. She tilts her head up towards mine. Her eyes are wide, unreadable. She is searching my face, trying to decide if I'll flinch again, and pull back, but I don't.

She reaches out, her hands curling around my arms, and steps in. I feel her weight shift forward, preparing to take the risk. Then her lips are on mine, soft, uncertain.

For a moment, I freeze, but then I react. My hands slide around her back, anchoring her to me. I've been waiting my whole life for this. Our kiss is light at first, slow, then it turns deeper, hungrier until I'm drowning in her. I am surrounded by her, her scent. Her warmth swallows me whole—until something shifts.

The air sharpens, pressure builds, a coldness threads through the edges of my awareness. A blanket wrapped around us. Close, deliberate, locking us in, allowing me to feel every touch, every caress, allowing the fire to burn hotter.

Then a warning. Ice under the skin, pressure at my temples. It jolts me back to the situation, our connection, and the realization that what is happening between Andy and me, our emotions and connection, may leak out to the others in the dorms.

Andy

I shiver.

But it's not from the kiss.

The kiss was heat, want, and clarity, the kind that makes everything around you disappear. Alex's mouth on mine, hands on my back, body pulling me in like I belonged there. It's what I have dreamed about forever.

No, this shiver is different.

This is not emptiness, but a cold layer, invisible and thick, a blanket of silence keeping the world out.

Alex tenses, not with fear, but with awareness.

"Shit," he breathes, pulling back just enough for his forehead to rest against mine, our breaths still tangled. His eyes search mine, and I see the realization there, too fast for me to brace for it.

"Mason," he exhales, jaw tight. "She's shielding us."

"Mason's... what?" I whisper, my voice cracking on the edge of disbelief. Shielding us? From what? From whom?

Shit, from Roarke, and the rest of the Wights, that's who.

From anyone tuned into our emotional network, in the overall shield cover.

The realization sinks like a stone. Mason felt it all. Instead of interrupting, she gave us space. "She's dampening your flare. Mine too. She felt something spike and dropped a block to keep others from sensing it. She's blocking us down from others."

I blink. The kiss. Our emotions. Everything that had been bottled up just exploded between us, and Mason felt it. She reacted, covering for us. Fast. Quietly.

Handled it, as she always does. To protect us.

I know Mason is always scanning, always watching out for the Wights, her family, friends more than others. That's the thing about her. She is everyone's protector or tries to be. Although she is several years from graduation, Mason hits X on every Tier; she is the strongest among us. She takes that responsibility seriously and uses her considerable Tier Two skills to keep a constant finger on the pulse around Elitus Campus.

But she just shielded Alex and me. We were exposed to others, especially my twin.

"Wait—so Roarke could've—?"

"He didn't. Thanks to Mason." Alex straightens, running a hand through his hair, the other lightly resting on my hip like he's afraid to let go too fast. "You know she always has feelers out. On me, on you, on the people she cares about."

I wrap my arms around myself, my thoughts racing. "I know, but you're her brother."

He smiles a soft, but sad, smile. I take a deep breath, the weight of it all crashing in at once. I feel frustrated, nervous, scared.

The shield cover, the kiss. Mason knows about her brother and I, and she gave us space, anyway. We had a moment, a real one. "What do we do now?" I whisper.

Alex's eyes go distant. The warmth vanishes and, in its place—duty. Guilt. The coldness seeps in. His face is a mask; his shoulders are tense again. The shift in him is sudden and unmistakable. He is withdrawing.

"I don't know," he says quietly. "I wish things were different. I want this, Andy. I do. But wanting isn't enough when everything is stacked against us. I don't know how to make this work."

The sting hits hard.

Because I have waited so long for this moment; for him. To see me. To finally let go. For us to be together.

But now?

I wish it had never happened. Because I know it won't happen again.

"I don't want to lead you on. I don't want to put you at risk," he adds, his voice barely above a whisper. He means it. Every word, but that doesn't make it easier.

"And I don't want you to walk away," I murmur, voicing my pain.

He flinches, and for a heartbeat, I see it. The want, the regret, the war behind his eyes; but he doesn't move.

Instead, I do.

I'll make it easy for him.

I take a step back, wrapping my arms around myself. To hold my heart in so I don't leave it shattered on the floor. "It's okay, Alex," I lie, because it's easier than asking him to choose something he's already convinced himself he can't have. "Thank you for tonight."

His hands curl into fists like he's fighting every instinct to reach for me again. But he doesn't.

And that tells me everything I need to know.

I turn before I lose my nerve. The shield Mason cast is still around us, a slight layer. I can feel it start to lift as I walk away. She gives me a chance to get myself level before she lifts it completely. To prevent Roarke, or anyone else, from picking up what I am feeling, what happened between us.

I open his door and shut it behind me. With a soft final click, I don't look back. Because if I do, I'll fall apart. I'll beg him to change his mind. When I know he won't.

The hallway is dim and silent. I take slow steps, trying to build up my resolve. I walk down the stairs to my first-floor room. Each step is harder than the last. It takes all my energy and focus not to crumble on the steps.

Right now, I wish I had never stopped by, never gone out. Those few brief hours meant everything to me. The time in his room, his lips on mine. His touch. It seemed like he didn't want to let me go.

But he did. He always will. I knew it, but I got lost in the fantasy, anyway.

The cold is still there around me. I know it's not meant to be evasive, but it still carries awareness. Her shield is a reminder that someone is always watching, always feeling for us.

I slip into my room, strip off my clothes, numb to the chill in the air, and climb beneath the covers. I curl into myself; arms wrapped around my pillow like it's the only solid thing left in my life. But no matter how tightly I hold it, I still feel the emptiness inside me. It hums beneath my skin.

I grab my phone, the screen too bright in the dark, and text Mason before I can overthink it.

Me: *Are you always watching?*

Her reply comes almost instantly.

Mason: *It's not really watching. I feel for spikes in emotions. Especially for my family and friends. Pain. Fear. Love. I can teach you how to shield more. You might be a lost cause like Charley, though*

.

I snort, despite the ache. That's such a Mason answer—sharp honestly softened with humor.

Me: *If you can, please! Shit... how does that work? He's your brother?*

Mason: *And you're one of my best friends. I won't tell you what I picked up from him, but I have to ask... How was your first kiss? LOL.*

I roll my eyes, but it's too late. The smile's already tugging at my lips. Just a little. A splinter of something good, something real, lodged in the wreckage of tonight.

Me: *You suck.... but thank you.*

There's a pause. Then:

Mason:*I believe in Fate, Andy.It's meant to be, just give it time.*

I stare at the screen, her words blurring.

Fate.

Do I believe in that?

I want to.

I want to believe tonight meant something.

That Alex's hand in mine, his lips on mine—wasn't just adrenaline or circumstance. That this aching, impossible thing between us matters. Even if he's not ready to admit it yet.

But belief is hard when you've spent most of your life feeling like you're too much and never enough.

Me: *I can try.*

I set the phone on my nightstand and lie back; the sheets cool against my skin; the silence settles around me. But it's not an empty silence.

It hums. With what was, with what might be, with Hope.

Not the kind that begs to be fulfilled, but the kind that refuses to die quietly.

I still hurt, ache, wish he'd chosen me tonight.

But more than anything, I hope I can be enough. For him. For us. For whatever comes next.

Six

Alex

The holidays pass by in a blur this year.

It could be the nonstop prep for the bar exam; I've been buried in flashcards for weeks, halfway through memorizing the penal code. Or maybe it's because I attempted to avoid the dorms, to avoid her. I've been splitting my time between the labs and the Elitus offices or home with my family, trying to convince myself that distance is the right call.

It doesn't help.

Not really.

Home is easy. Kennedy, all three feet of unchecked energy, basically rules the Clarke House now. Four years old, soon to be five, she's a holiday tyrant with sparkly boots and a strong opinion about reindeer. Our moms go all-out for Christmas, but Mason and Mya took it further this year. It looks like Santa's sleigh exploded in our living room.

No one minds.

Christmas morning is loud, bright, and sticky with sugar from Mason's homemade donuts. Kennedy insists I sit next to her during presents—she says it's "so I can open the hard ones," but I know better. She wants an audience for her joy, and I'm happy to play along.

Later in the afternoon, we head to the James house. It's a tradition now that half of the combat team shows up. Roarke and Andy roll in not long after we do, Andy in a red sweater with silver snowflakes and a smile that's almost too wide to be real.

I can't look at her for very long.

Bastian, Kyle, and the Ross twins show up with Charley in tow, arms full of gifts and desserts. Everyone knows my mom's holiday table is epic, so no one's surprised Wyatt and

Kate make an appearance. Music, board games, and an alarming amount of competitive card-playing in which Kyle loses, despite cheating.

It's a great night of friendship and family.

Warm. Easy. Familiar. And yet... I feel like a ghost.

Andy laughs, two chairs down from me. I know she feels the wall I've rebuilt between us because I can't meet her eyes for more than a second. And I hate it. But I can't bring it down, not when everything tells me that stepping closer will cost us more than we can afford.

She's been quiet too. Not cold, just... gone. Giving me space. Like we both agreed to not mention the fire we started between us.

It's hard when we are together to act like everything is okay.

I smile at the right moments, keep the conversation light, and pretend the weight pressing into my ribs isn't her absence.

It's a relief when the night winds down. But when she walks out without looking back? It buries itself deep. Like I deserve it.

The week between Christmas and the Winter Ball is busy. Meetings. Field readiness updates. Legal summaries. I took my exam months earlier than McGuire was ready for. We have to wait for the results, but I already know I did well. For now, I am slotted as an aide in the contract office, not exactly thrilling. A glorified translator between the legal, political, and military branches. But it's something, a place to start pulling threads.

I'm combat-enabled and still certified to lead Tier One and Two missions, but they've kept me benched. When I get sent out, I ensure I'm paired with Roarke and Andy. Because if I can't talk to her, I can at least make sure she comes home.

It's the kind of logic that would drive her insane if she knew. But it's all I have left.

Andy

If perfection had a scent, it would be the Winter Ball.

There's glitter in the air, actual glitter, suspended in soft, shimmery bursts that catch the icy-blue lights like snowflakes frozen mid-fall. The Academy's main hall is unrecognizable. Where there are usually chairs and tables, mats, and training equipment; now there are white linens, candles in crystal holders, and long tables of food, none of us will remember eating.

It's beautiful. Elegant.

And fake.

At least for me.

I'm wearing midnight blue floor-length satin with a low back and silver threading across the bodice that Mason picked out with an evil grin. I look the part, my hair's curled, my makeup on point, and I fix a megawatt smile on my face.

But inside? I'm unraveling. No matter how much I smile or how loud I laugh, Alex hasn't looked at me all night.

I clock him early on. Dark suit, his hair styled, his face a portrait of calm and controlled perfection. He's off to the side most of the night. Chatting with everyone, cool and collected. Riddick and his family, as usual, are in Aspen, so Alex and Roarke stand and chat with Kyle, Max, and Bastian throughout the evening.

He dances with his sisters and moms, then is back in the corner like a statue. A statue that won't meet my eyes.

I'm not surprised. But that doesn't make it hurt less.

I down my first drink too quickly, hoping the bubbles would fill the space in my chest where hope used to live. They don't.

"He's staring," Mya murmurs beside me, nudging her elbow into mine. Alex's sister is a spitfire, the youngest female in the dorms.

I force a grin and spin toward her, glass raised. "At the drink table?"

"At you," she retorts, calm as ever. "He has been for the last ten minutes."

I chance a glance. He's not staring now, but his jaw's clenched, and his posture's rigid.

"He won't come over," I say, voice flat.

"Should he have to?" Charley asks, sliding into our little circle with a drink in each hand. She hands me a fresh one. "You could just walk up to him and say, 'Hey, remember when you kissed me like I was oxygen?'"

Charley's comment lands like a grenade. I nearly choke on the first sip. "Jesus, Charley." I glare at her, but it's too late—the reminder flashes in my mind.

She winks. Charley is as wild and vibrant as you would expect, a redhead who wields the power of fire. Her Firestarter nickname has been there forever. She literally is firepower in human form. She has always been Mason's bestie, but over the years, they let me into their inner circle. Charley is all wisecracks, power hits, and polished beauty. She works out and maintains a figure that anyone would die for. Curves for days, her fashion style borders between sexy glam and edgy girl next-door vibes. Tonight is no different, a gray and black low cut, high-slit gown that showcases her ample cleavage, while the open, low drape of the back shows off her physique that comes from hours in the gym with Mason.

"She's right," Mya says. "You could just talk to him." I give them both a look. After being depressed about the whole situation, I spilled the beans to my two besties one night. Which, of course, meant that Mya, Siobhan, and the Ross twins, Charley's older sisters, Marty and Paige, were also in on the secret. Basically, the whole female combat squad other than Kate.

I hoped getting it off my chest would help me forget, move on. But it didn't. I remember every second of warmth. Before, cold shields and excuses swallowed it.

It's been weeks. I haven't pressed him. I haven't even tried. It's been cold every night since, but nothing like that one night. Nothing like the chill that came after his lips left mine.

I've just waited. Silently. Stupidly. Wondering if maybe he'd remember too.

The one person I want to pull me close is standing across the room like the space between us is where he means to stay. Maybe it's time I stopped waiting.

The Ball bleeds into the after-party, and everything blurs. The glitter fades, the music shifts, and I drift. Room to room, conversation to conversation, smiling when I should, laughing when I must. But it all feels like background noise to the static in my chest.

Alex keeps his word; we have a party. But it stays calm, at least on the surface. Laughter filters through the common area, liquor flows, and someone puts on a playlist that's too loud, but cheerful. I hear the Happy Birthdays given to Mason, since the Ball always falls on New Year's Eve, and her birthday is New Year's Day.

Alex walks in sometime later.

And just like that, the breath leaves my lungs.

He's still in his suit, jacket off, tie loose, shirt sleeves rolled up. He looks tired, guarded, and beautiful in a way that makes my stomach twist. For a second, the crowd parts. I see him. He sees me. The pull that is always there when we are close tugs hard.

But he doesn't come closer.

My pulse stumbles. I wait for a beat too long before I turn away, forcing myself not to react. If I stay in his orbit one more second, I'll do something I will regret.

Mason catches my eye across the room, her expression unreadable.

I can't help but wonder... how much does she feel? Does she know?

I don't ask. Because I already know what she'd say.

Give it time. Hold on. Believe in Fate.

But time feels heavier than it used to. As if it's something I'm dragging behind me instead of moving through. It stretches, strains, and stays empty: the space between Alex and me.

So, I fake one more smile. I pretend everything is okay. When you don't have answers, and you don't have control, sometimes pretending is the only thing you can do.

Despite that, beneath the ache, the doubt, I feel it.

A spark. The pull is still there. And with it, a sliver of hope that maybe he's still pretending too.

SEVEN

Andy

I am not sure when the ache turned into anger. Maybe it has been building for a while—simmering under the surface, hiding beneath all the forced smiles and fake calm and all the bullshit I keep feeding myself.

It's fine. I am fine. That I don't care.

But I do.

And now? I'm tired of pretending.

It's been nearly three months since our diner date. A month since the Winter Ball, and I am over trying to be the strong one, the good one. Hoping maybe he will come to me again.

So, when Roarke mentions a late-night recon sweep: minimal risk, secondary porter needed, I volunteer before he finishes his sentence. I don't care; I need to move; to do something, to fight something. To burn off all this wild energy that courses beneath my skin.

But when we enter the war room, I see him. Just my fucking luck. Alex hardly runs missions anymore, too busy dealing with contracts and the inner workings of Elitus, its legal, and military branches.

He's already waiting, geared up and ready to go. Next to Max, his brother, who notices me first. Then Alex's eyes lift to mine, and I look away. I don't want to see it: the regret, the need that he pretends isn't there.

I know, no matter what, he won't bend.

He won't break Elitus' precious rules.

It drives me insane.

The mission is supposed to be routine. A recon sweep, low contact probability. Quick in and out to verify movement near one of the old PPG labs. The type of assignment you run in your sleep.

But from the second we go, I know it's not routine for Alex.

He hasn't looked at me once. Not during the initial rundown, the briefing. I followed the orders. No jokes. No eye contact.

But I still feel it.

The way his energy shifts whenever I move. The way his jaw clenches when I port ahead to scout, even though I follow the damn plan to the letter. He says nothing, but he doesn't have to. His silence says enough. He's pissed that I am even here.

Roarke is unusually muted, too. He's sticking close, more observant than normal. Not overbearing. But he is watching me. He knows I'm seconds away from throwing myself into something dangerous to feel alive.

When Alex doesn't look at me, when he pretends I don't matter; it wrecks me.

Max is Max. The Quiet One. Laid-back, sharp, and focused. He catches my eye once when I move ahead to check a blind corner. He doesn't say it, but his brows lift just enough to let me know he clocked my mood. And he is thinking the same thing as Roarke; I'm being reckless, pushing it, unraveling again.

But I don't care.

Out here, I'm still doing something useful.

I'm not the girl Alex keeps walking away from; not someone's sister, someone's mistake. I am a combat-enabled Tier Three operative who has a purpose and is important to the mission's success.

The entry goes smoothly. Roarke cleared the upper area, with Max on the perimeter. I port to the secondary wing, confirming it is empty. Nothing but dust, decay, and old tech stripped clean years ago. I drop back into formation, my breath steady, adrenaline muted.

It's a textbook mission. Well, except for the tension crackling between me and Alex.

"West sector is clear," I report, stepping beside Alex. He doesn't even glance my way, not even a nod. Just a clipped. "Copy."

And that?

That's it.

That's all it takes to snap the last thread of my restraint. I turn, my voice low but sharp. "Is there a problem, Alex?"

"No."

"You seem to have a problem with me out here."

"You shouldn't have to be out here," he says, quiet but lethal.

I laugh, bitter and brightly. "But I am."

"Doesn't mean I have to like it," he mutters.

Roarke and Max are waiting for us as we move forward. They are pretending not to hear us, giving us space, giving Alex space to walk away from me. Again.

"Sucks, doesn't it?" I ask, smiling at him as we reach the others. "That you don't get to control me."

He looks at me, then passes a look to my twin. "I don't want to control you, Andy."

"It sure feels like it."

"Are we good?" Roarke asks, trying to end whatever is escalating.

"We're perfect," I say, sarcasm like poison. I glance at Alex, and this time he's looking back. He knows what's coming.

Because I am angry now.

And when I'm angry?

That's when the shit hits the fan.

Alex

Fucking Andy.

She's been distant for weeks, and I have no one to blame but myself.

I thought I was doing the right thing, keeping my distance. I know Riddick warned me to be honest, but it's too hard. Because every time I am near her, she breaks my resolve. And I want to say fuck it, and take what I want, what my entire system is yearning for. But I don't.

I thought I was protecting her.

Protecting us.

Especially after Mason threw a docket at me, not long after my last mission with her. One about bonds, and the theory about connections caused by Agent X. A link between mated pairs. I get what she was trying to tell me. That it isn't just an attraction, that it's some type of cosmic pull, something meant to be. Fate.

But my resolve to stay away is getting harder. Andy doesn't look at me the same way anymore. If she does, it's from across a room, her expression unreadable—casual. Like we were never anything but glances and professional interactions.

It kills me.

Because I feel like I am standing still. Stuck. Wanting her more than I should. And that kiss? It made everything so much harder. Having her in my arms for those few minutes rerouted my entire system. Now, I can't even look at another.

I've thought about approaching my father, Elitus, and asking them to change the rules, and then I think about what it will mean. And I lose my nerve.

Because what I'm considering? It will change everything.

Rules, assignments, missions, training, our command structure. Not just my life, but also hers, my siblings, my friends. Everyone. And everything.

Since our last mission, she has been pushing harder than ever. It shows how little control I have over anything in my life.

The worst was when I heard through the rumor mill about how she went off base with Mason for a "history" project. Without an escort. I could've wrung their necks. I get it, the rebellion, but neither of them thinks about the risk. It makes my skin crawl, and my agitation morphs to dangerous levels.

Andy and I argued. Loudly. About protocol. About how dangerous it was; how stupidly reckless and immature it was. She'd accused me of being controlling. I'd told her I didn't want to find her body in a ditch.

She lost it. And how does she pay me back?

By getting drunk two nights later at Gen Three's nineteenth birthday party and flirting with every guy in the dorms like she's got something to prove. She wants to twist the knife just a little deeper. Roarke even pulled me aside that night, his voice low with a warning: "You don't get to screw her up, Alex. Not like this."

I didn't answer. Because what was I supposed to say? Too late?

And Mason? Mason has not been easy to deal with. She's on every roster, training in all three tiers. Running herself into the ground; most days she looks like hell.

Today was no different. She trained from early morning to late afternoon: classroom, mental Tier Two exercises, field maneuvers, and power stamina drills. By the time she hit the mat for weapons, she looked wrecked. But of course, she didn't stop. She never stops. Then she made it to Kyle in Tier Three training.

I agreed when McGuire suggested she step back, hoping that hearing it from me would have an influence.

Instead?

The look she gave me was as if I had betrayed her. Her face went stony. Her voice clipped. Then she walked out without another word.

This wasn't always the case.

Mason used to be... light. Intense, sure, but sharp and present. Now, it's like she's bleeding herself out by inches, trying to prove she's invincible. And we: Riddick, Kyle, Bastian, Roarke, and I, we let her. We treated her as a weapon. A resource. Something too valuable to rest.

Now, she'd rather burn out completely than let anyone take that choice away.

I can't win with the women in my life.

Andy avoids me, Mason resents me, and my mother asked me last week if I've "been sleeping at all" in that tone that says she already knows the answer and doesn't like it.

EIGHT

Alex

Tonight's mission was short and clean, tactical recon and security sweep near the southern border. I took Mason's place, partnering with Riddick, Kyle, and Roarke. I led the squad. We were in and out in under two hours.

Textbook. Still, I barely said ten words the whole time. It's late, midnight. I should go to my room, maybe crack open a file or two before bed. But my feet take me to the girls' floor, passing Max and Bastian in the common area.

The way Mason looked at me today, like I was McGuire's shadow—still sits like acid in my gut. I knock on her door; she doesn't answer.

I wait half a beat, then push it open. Her bed is made, training gear folded at the edge, no light, no music; just empty. It hits like a gut punch.

Mason didn't go home. She's not in the dorms or labs. And I'm no longer thinking like the Elitus liaison or the mission leader; but like a concerned brother.

I already know what happened. They ported. Off base. On their own. Without an escort. My jaw tightens.

I hear voices downstairs—Roarke, Riddick, Kyle, returning and updating Max and Bastian. They are all lounging in the main area.

Still in full gear, I descend the steps, tension winding tighter with every one of them.

I walk into the common room like a loaded gun.

"Can you read her?" I snap, locking eyes with Riddick, who is on the couch, unlacing his boots.

"She's been blocking all day," he says, looking up with a frown. "Why?"

"She and her hellion partner are MIA."

He and I exchange a look, and the fire that's been simmering inside me all week flares hot.

"I'm going to fucking kill her."

Before anyone can respond, Andy comes down the hall.

She's in leggings and an oversized sweatshirt, hair still damp from a shower, eyes sharp. When she spots the look on my face, she laughs.

That laugh, mocking, dismissive, and daring.

"What did you think they'd do, Alex? Sit in their rooms and eat bonbons?" Andy crosses her arms like she's not standing ten feet from a powder keg. "You've all spent the entire week calling them unworthy. I hope they're having a drink for me, too."

I step toward her before I can stop myself, but Roarke's already there. His hand hits my chest, firm, grounding. He doesn't push but holds me there. He knows I'm close to blurting out something I can't take back.

"Back down," he warns. "She's goading you. And she should know better." He turns to her, his tone shifting. "Where are they, Andy?"

"They're out," she says with a shrug, feigning innocence. "I don't know exactly where. But judging by their outfits, they will make a few guys swallow their tongues."

The entire room is tense. Kyle sits up straighter. Bastian stops with his drink almost at his lips. Even Riddick's jaw flexes. Andy smirks, all sharp edges and satisfaction.

"What time?" I grind out.

She glances at the clock. "About three hours ago. Don't worry. Mason said she'd see me at breakfast."

I turn to Kyle. "Can you get Charley?"

He opens his mouth—but Bastian beats him to it. "No," he says, voice cool. "Mason's shielding. Hard. Feels like she's blocking for both."

My hands curl into fists. "Get David," I say tightly to Max. "Maybe he can trace them."

Andy doesn't move. She watches me, eyes bright with defiance. She's glowing with satisfaction, feeding off my fury like its oxygen.

The tension in the room is suffocating. Heavy with everything we're not saying. Andy leans against the wall like a damn flame, taunting me with her smirk. The one that says, how's your control now?

Mason and Charley are still gone. The air feels electric, but not in a good way—it's like we're all one spark away from detonation.

And Mason? She's daring me to light the match. She's been uncontrollable for weeks, but tonight it's different. Intentional. If she pushes McGuire one inch further, he will get what he's wanted for months—her out of the program. Off the team. Out of combat.

I should be furious. And I am. But underneath that heat, something that sinks deep in my chest and settles hard. Fear.

When David Owens finally stumbles in, looking like Max yanked him straight out of REM sleep. His dark curls are a mess, his hoodie still half on, half clinging to one arm.

"Sup?" he mutters, his voice scratchy with exhaustion.

"Can you trace a sat phone?" I cut to the point.

David blinks. "Yeah, sure. Who's missing?"

Across the room, Andy lets out a sharp laugh. That sound grates like broken glass being dragged across metal. She's still watching me as if this is some show she paid for.

Roarke gives her a look, but she doesn't flinch. She doesn't care; she keeps watching.

"Mason and Charley are off-grid. They're shielding; both are blocked." My voice comes out clipped. "I'm calling Mason's sat phone. Get ready to trace. I need a location."

David nods, cracking his knuckles and mentally focusing one hand on the cell phone. "Sixty seconds. Just give me something."

I dial and hit the speaker. The line rings.

And then—music. Loud. Throbbing bass. Laughter. Voices. The background noise explodes through the speaker, turning the quiet dorm into a vibrating echo chamber.

I feel my jaw tic. My grip tightens on the glass. I start the mental countdown.

"Yes?" she says, breathless, still laughing.

"Where are you?" I bark.

"Out," she replies breezily. "Letting off steam. As instructed."

"Mason, get back here. Now."

"Or what?" Her tone sharpens. Defensive. "Are you going to scold me? You had your chance, Alex. If any of you gave a damn, maybe you would've stood up for me. But no, go on—be Daddy's good little soldier. You can even borrow Kyle's cape for the day."

The room goes dead silent. Riddick freezes halfway through, cracking his neck. Kyle stops pacing. And I feel every eye shift to me. Mason's words aren't just a jab. They're a shot through the heart. I close my eyes and inhale.

"Mason," I say low, a warning. "Don't do this."

Her voice comes back over the line; her tone is mixed with anger and regret. "Too late," she says. "Oh, and by the way? David's good... but I'm better."

The line goes dead.

The room crackles. Static burst from the phone, loud and sharp, destroying it. David stumbles back, one hand to his head as if someone just threw a live wire through his skull.

"Fuck—" He groans. "I don't know how she pulled that off," he mutters. But he stands up and tries to recalibrate himself. "Okay. West Coast. LA or Vegas, maybe. I can't get tighter than that without a better anchor."

Kyle's already moving, bringing his phone out. "Can you go again?"

David swears but nods, still blinking through the mental feedback. "Thirty seconds, tops."

Kyle doesn't wait. He dials. Charley answers on the second ring, sounding way too pleased.

"What, Kyle?" she purrs. "You coming to get us? Or just Mason? Because right now, she's dancing with three guys who are very into it."

I see red. Andy shifts at the edge of my vision, smug satisfaction radiating off her like perfume. She doesn't say a word; she doesn't have to. Her eyes say it all.

Before Charley can hang up, Kyle and Riddick port out. I swear and throw back the rest of my drink. My hands are shaking.

"You going to storm in after them, knight in shining armor?" Andy asks, tilting her head. "Or is Daddy's golden boy just going to sit back and let someone else clean it up for him?"

That's it. I slam the glass onto the table hard enough to crack it. The sound cuts through the room like a gunshot.

My hands curl into fists at my sides. I glance at her, really get a good look at her, and there it is, right beneath the anger, the sarcasm, the pokes, and prods.

She's hurting. She's furious. But not just at me. At everything.

At how I let her get close, how I pulled away, how I pretended that none of it mattered. The lack of control over her life makes her feel trapped.

I shake my head. Her lips part in a breathless laugh, sad eyes, and anger at the situation. At me. "Coward."

I don't flinch. I turn to David instead. "You got it?" He nods and gives Roarke the coordinates. But even as I say it, I feel her eyes on me. She is watching me, and that pisses me off more than anything else tonight. No matter how many rules I follow, or how tightly I grip control, she still gets to me.

Every. Damn. Time.

Andy

The room is quiet, the air a little less tense, once they are gone. No more barbs. Just silence—and the sound of me being left behind.

Alex. Roarke. Kyle. Riddick.

Gone in a blink, out chasing down Mason and Charley, like it's an emergency.

Mason didn't ask to be saved. She asked to be seen. And no one listened.

I exhale the adrenaline racing through me, leaving a bitter taste in my mouth. The common room is quieter now, but the tension has gone nowhere. It just hangs there, like smoke after a fire, thick and uncomfortable.

David mutters something under his breath, still rubbing the side of his head from whatever psychic backlash Mason slammed into his skull. Max offers him a bottle of water, and I hear murmurs from the others, but it's all background noise now.

Because I'm still thinking about him. I shouldn't have pushed Alex like that. But I couldn't help it. The moment I saw the look on his face, like he was back in control, on his high moral ground, as Elitus' golden son. I snapped. And Mason, her comments? She feels it too.

As mad as I am over the bullshit sexist treatment, the worst part is I wanted him to hurt. To be hurt like I have been. Hurt because that's what I have been feeling for months. I know I came off like a brat. I wanted to piss him off. But what else am I supposed to do?

I lean back and close my eyes, trying to shake the memory, but it's already there, vivid and unforgiving. Alex's fingers threaded with mine. The weight of his gaze, the way his breath caught right before he kissed me. The way my heart felt, like it had finally stopped searching for something. No matter how hard I try to forget the memory, I can't.

The tension between us is still a live wire. We're one second away from combusting. It's exhausting and impossible to avoid.

I swipe at my eyes, angry they're wet. My fingers curl around the couch cushion like it's the only thing keeping me together.

A sharp pain lodges itself behind my ribs. I don't want to cry. I won't cry. So, I breathe, I straighten. I pull myself back together because that's what I always do. What Roarke taught me, what Elitus demands.

Sensing my issues, Max takes a seat next to me. The Quiet One, always silent, but helpful. He's a decent Tier Two. I feel him trying to calm me. All I can do is give him a sad smile.

Because inside, I'm splintering. It's too hard. The distance makes the ache so much worse; it seems like I am the only one suffering; it makes me angry.

"He doesn't mean to hurt you," Max says quietly. "Trust me, he cares, Andy. Otherwise, he wouldn't react the way he does."

"Does it even matter anymore?" I murmur to Max.

"Do you want it too?"

"I want to matter to him. More than just a Wight under his command. Am I a woman or a weapon?"

"Can't you be both?" he turns to face me. "I know I don't have an inside track to Elitus, but this can't continue forever. You must decide what you want and if you will fight for it."

"I am fighting." More tears stream down my face. "I am so tired of fighting, how I feel, what I want, how he acts, his need to control everything. Pretending everything is okay. Pretending I'm okay. It's so exhausting." Max grabs my hand, sending more calming vibes my way.

"You are okay," he murmurs. "Alex will not change Andy. He is proud and loyal. He's controlling to a point, but he is reasonable. Even if the rules change, he will still be Alex. Is that what you want?"

"He's all I've ever wanted," I whisper. Max nods and pulls me into a sideways hug. Comforting me. The gentle giant, who cares too much sometimes.

But I wonder—when they return, when I see Alex again, will he say something?

Or will he realize maybe I'm not what he wants after all?

Alex

Through the flashing neon lights and pulsing bass, I spot them; Mason and Charley, dead center on the dance floor, surrounded by a crowd of gawking men.

Defiant. Unbothered. Drawing way too much attention.

Mason looks sober but furious. Charley is half-wasted, draped over one guy while another whispers in her ear.

My shoulders tighten with tension. This is reckless, even for them.

Roarke and I push through the crowd, cutting toward them as the scene unfolds in real time.

"This isn't a mission or the arena, Kyle. I don't take orders from you," Mason snaps, her voice razor-sharp and unwavering. Her eyes locked on Kyle, who looks two seconds away from throwing her over his shoulder and dragging her out himself.

"But you will from me," my voice cuts through the noise as I grab her arm. "Let's go."

I hold my grip firm, but not forceful. "Please."

Mason hesitates. A flicker of something—conflict, maybe—crosses her face before she exhales sharply and nods. She may be furious, but she knows this isn't the time or place to argue.

Charley grins, wiggling her fingers in a lazy, half-hearted wave at her admirers before following.

Before I can process what's happening, Riddick gives the firm command: Move.

In an instant, we're going, cutting toward the emergency exit, slipping through it in a blur, porting out before anyone even notices.

Back home, Mason doesn't say a word. She blows past us and heads straight upstairs, shoulders tight, movements rigid. I meet Riddick's gaze. He nods, confirming what I already suspect.

PPG.

Goddamn it. Now I have to bring this to Elitus.

We crossed the line tonight. And I'm not sure I can pull her back from it.

NINE

"Mason, you put many people in danger yesterday. You drew unnecessary attention just because you didn't get what you wanted. Someone could've gotten hurt, or worse," Dr. Ross drones, his tone flat and rehearsed. To him, she's a nuisance and a problem.

After a sleepless night, I brought it to my father. He may oversee the program overall, but day-to-day operations, training, discipline, enforcement, that's Ross and McGuire. And today, they've made Mason the target. The punishment will be severe, but what that means, I don't know. No missions? Additional training? We haven't had this happen, not at this level, before.

I hate we are here, where she is the one on trial. I didn't justify her stunt, but I tried to shift the blame for pushing her there. Not that anyone wanted to hear it.

"Really? Me?" Mason fires back, sarcasm dripping. "Cause I'm pretty damn sure I was out there for four hours before they even noticed. Never mind that your golden boys over there showed up unshielded and uncloaked. They drew the PPG's attention—not me."

"You know you're not to go out without an escort," Stephen—Riddick's father—says, voice clipped.

"An escort. This shit again?" Mason scoffs, arms crossing. "Isn't that rich? I can run you and McGuire's little side missions' solo, but if I hit a club without a babysitter, it's bad form?"

The room goes still, and everyone feels the air shift. That slow, suffocating tension pressing in from all sides. My pulse kicks up, dread curling in my gut. What the hell is she talking about? I glance at my father. He looks just as blindsided.

Mason laughs, low and lethal. She knows exactly what she's done. She set off a bomb, and now she's standing back to watch the room explode.

"Oops, did I let your secret out?" She turns, eyes sweeping over me, Riddick, Kyle—every single one of us. "That's right, boys. Y'all think I've had nights off? Wrong. I do the shit McGuire needs to be done but doesn't want Elitus to know about. Solo. No backup. No lifeline. Nothing. Still think I need to be benched?"

Her words hit like a punch to the gut. My temper spikes to a level I never fucking knew I had. My head snaps to McGuire. Then Stephen. Then Nick. She's not lying. And even if she were... Mason doesn't bluff about shit like this.

Dad's face goes pale, his voice tightening as he turns on his peers. "Is she serious? You have her running missions alone?"

Silence.

Thick. Damning. The kind that confirms everything without a single word.

"Mason." Dad's voice is all wrong—too low, too sharp. And damn.... Now I know where I got it from. "Why didn't you come to me?"

Mason lets out a hollow, humorless laugh. "Oh, now you want to be Daddy?" Her voice shakes, something raw, barely held in check. "It's a little late to play that role. Fuck you. I'm done." She shakes her head. "Do what you want. If I'm too dangerous, too unstable, too uncontrolled—or sloppy, or whatever the hell you want to call me—then fine. Bench me. Bench me forever. Just don't come to me for your bullshit. I'm done helping any of you."

I see it now—what I should've seen long ago. Mason is not just pissed.

She's exhausted. Bone-deep, soul-crushing exhaustion.

She's spent years proving herself, pushing harder, working longer, and never being given the same leash the rest of us take for granted.

No one carries more; no one is asked for more. And she's often told she's not enough. That she needs to be managed, controlled, and contained.

She locks eyes with McGuire, daring him to push her. He takes the bait.

"Don't threaten me, young lady." His voice cuts sharply. "You won't just be benched—you'll be out."

Something flickers across her face too fast for most to catch it. But I do.

A split-second of devastation; of loss. Gone as quickly as it came, buried beneath the steel in her eyes, beneath the recklessness that always follows when she's pushed too far.

She lifts her chin. "Do it," she says, voice like ice. "See where I end up."

Holy shit.

"Mason, you don't mean that." I cut in quickly, trying to stop this before it goes any further.

The implication is clear; she doesn't mean it. She would never go to Dmitri. Never the PPG.

She won't say it, but she fears him. But McGuire doesn't know that, and he wouldn't hesitate to make an example out of her, and she knows it.

Part of me wonders if she's pushing to see if he'll give the order.

"Of course not, Alex," she says smoothly, her voice light, mocking. "Robert would never let them kick me out. Mom would kill him."

Nick Thompson has had enough. "You're off rotation. For at least a month. Get yourself in check—and your hormones."

Mason doesn't argue; she doesn't flinch. She turns on her heel and walks out, leaving wreckage in her wake.

But I see it just before she disappears. The tremble in her fingers, the hitch in her breath. She won't break in front of them; she never does.

But she's not okay.

And we let her get to this point.

The second she's gone, chaos erupts. Elitus' heads break into a full-scale argument.

Max shifts into damage control, murmuring with Kyle, trying to keep things from completely blowing up.

I register nothing else. Just Riddick storming out, fury radiating off him like heat.

I don't hesitate. I follow, brushing past Maria and Joanne outside the doors. They don't stop me. They know better.

"Riddick, wait."

I grab his arm, but he yanks away hard enough to knock me off balance.

"Not now, Alex. I'm about to blow. I need the boot."

I get it. I feel it too. So, I let him lead the way.

The boot doors open, and I'm already yanking off my shirt, shifting mid-stride.

There's no pain anymore. No hesitation. Just the smooth transition from skin to steel; like slipping into another version of myself.

The weight settles over me like armor, my body gleaming beneath the harsh training lights.

I've worked damn hard to make my transformation this flawless.

It may not be the flashiest ability, but when I need to be a weapon...

I am pure force, an immovable object, a living blade.

We hit the boot and clash immediately. Riddick already summoned his weapon of choice, although we both will use hand to hand as well.

It's nicknamed the boot because no one steps on its floors without lacing up. It's our main battle arena; it demands blood, grit, and control.

Riddick's all muscle and unfiltered rage. He doesn't need fancy abilities or high-tier powers; his body is a weapon. Forged through years of brutal and relentless training.

Every strike he lands feels like a sledgehammer. And for a guy of his size, his speed is unnerving.

But me? I meet him head-on, steel against skin.

My reinforced frame absorbs the blows without budging. And when I swing, I hit just as hard—harder when I want to.

Sweat, blood, pure unchecked force.

We move in a brutal rhythm; blow for blow, never yielding.

We know each other's tells, our patterns.

It's chess at full throttle, counter and counterstrike, strategy buried beneath instinct.

Every punch I land echoes through the boot, vibration crawling up my metal limbs.

But Riddick doesn't flinch. He absorbs the impact like a goddamn tank, feeding off it, driving forward, never yielding.

The worst part about it is that he isn't using his abilities. No boosts, no enhancements. Just brute strength and discipline.

He's holding back, same as me.

Because we both know what happens if we don't. That's what scares us most.

After an hour, we stop, panting, bruised, still buzzed from the fight.

I grab my phone, my frown deepening when I see a text from Mom.

She's pissed, but she's cleaned up some of the mess.

"Did you know?" I ask, voice tight. Obviously, his dad was aware of Mason's extra missions.

"Absolutely not," he growls. "If I had, she would've never gone out solo. I'm so fucking pissed at him right now. She's not ready, not for that. They might think she is, but she's not."

"My father is losing his shit, too. McGuire will hopefully lie low. But God—her fucking mouth." I scrub my hand over my face. "If you get the order, I need to know. I don't care what it costs. She's my sister."

Riddick looks at me, face unreadable.

I know it's crossed his mind.

McGuire might need Mason, but his ego is the biggest liability in the room. Nobody challenges him and walks away unscathed.

"You don't have to worry about that," Riddick says. "If McGuire gives the order, he's a dead man. It doesn't matter whom he asks. We've already discussed it."

A flicker of relief, short-lived.

"My bigger worry is the side missions," Riddick mutters. "He could set her up, send her with a weak squad, make her the target. Using mid-tier collateral, especially if he thinks she's a threat."

"So, what can we do?"

"Honestly? Not much. Unless we speed up her training," he exhales sharply, dragging a hand over his short-cropped hair. "She already knows. She's been hiding from everyone for a while now. If she does, she can drop off his radar. She can be Robert's Mia. That's the best advice I've got. You're the only one she might listen to. She's too pissed at me and Kyle. She's off rotation for at least a month."

"She's out of training too," I add, watching his jaw tighten.

We both know she won't lie low; she takes a challenge almost as badly as he does.

Riddick exhales through his nose, shaking his head.

"She shouldn't have to fight this hard, you know?" His voice dips lower, heavier. "She acts like she doesn't care, but she does. She always does."

I study him. The way he tenses when she's mentioned. The way his jaw ticks when she does something dangerous. Much like me, he cares more than he's willing to admit.

"You could tell her that," I say.

He lets out a dry, bitter chuckle. "And what? Give her another reason to push back?" He shakes his head. "Nah. It's better she thinks I'm just another asshole trying to control her."

I frown. "That's bullshit, and you know it."

He shrugs, rubbing his knuckles. "Doesn't change the truth. It's easier this way. I need her safe more than I need to be with her."

I let out a slow breath and nod.

I get it; I do. She may be my sister, but Riddick would take a bullet for her. He is her shield on missions, and here on campus. Although he may train her hard, he looks out for her; he cares for her.

But he is right. Mason is at risk now more than ever.

"My mom texted," I say, steering the conversation. "Maria and she are livid—especially at Robert. They pulled her out. 'Let her enjoy being a nineteen-year-old girl,' was the quote I got. Wyatt will help her finish up the coursework she's behind on. She'll still need to purge power, though. Otherwise, she's going to be drunk for the next month."

Riddick snorts. "Yeah. She'll figure something out."

I nod, rolling out my stiff shoulders. "I'll talk to her."

When she lets me, that is. I know my comment yesterday lit the fuse.

I've got work to do, fixing whatever I've been screwing up with her.

Screwing up with everyone, it seems.

Riddick updates me on a few things his dad said. He promises to talk to him, maybe even with McGuire, making sure Mason at least has backup.

We're not stupid. We both know that whatever he's got her doing needs to run. But that doesn't mean she has to do it alone.

Andy

I hear about it before I even see her.

The news spreads fast, whispers curling through the dorms like wildfire. Mason's off rotation. Alex took it to Robert. McGuire and Ross came down on her hard.

And then?

Then she detonated.

No one knows exactly what she said, but the aftermath paints a clear picture—Mason, standing in the middle of a room full of Elitus brass, throwing every dirty secret back in their faces. Calling out McGuire. Calling out Stephen. Saying things that could get her kicked out. Or worse.

That's what worries me. Not the fact that she snapped. I expected that. Hell, she's wound so tight, it was only a matter of time before she exploded.

But McGuire? He doesn't take threats lightly. And Mason just handed him a loaded weapon.

I need to find her.

I take the stairs two at a time, pulse drumming in my ears.

The halls are too quiet; the air is thick with something unspoken. People glance as I pass; some curious, others wary. They know I'm looking for her. No one seems to know where she went.

But I already know. She's hiding, which means she's in her room... or at her parents'.

I try her room, knocking once before pushing the door open. Empty. I swallow hard, trying to fight the twist in my gut. I don't like this. Not at all.

Mason doesn't hide. She fights. She argues. She throws punches.

But she doesn't disappear. Unless this time...it was too much.

I yank out my phone and dial before I can second-guess it.

It rings twice—voicemail.

I try again. Nothing.

Cursing under my breath, I spin on my heel and head back downstairs, scanning for Alex, Mya, or Max, anyone who might know where she went.

There were no signs of them. I grit my teeth. I need answers. Fast.

I scroll through my contacts and hit Aimee's name. She picks up almost immediately.

"Andy?" Her voice is cautious.

"Where is she?" I don't bother with pleasantries. Aimee hesitates. That's all I need to know. She knows.

"She's home." I sit down hard on my bed, exhaling.

"She left right after the meeting. Mom brought her to Dad's," Aimee says, sighing. "Mom is trying to talk to her, but I don't know if Mason's listening."

That tells me everything. She's at the Clarkes, but Joanne is trying to reach her—Maria and Robert must be dealing with the fallout. Or trying to.

Mason doesn't go home, not unless there's nowhere else to go. I tighten my grip on the phone. "Is she okay?"

"She says she is," Aimee replies, then pauses. "But you know, Mason. If she's not okay, she won't admit it."

I close my eyes and rub my forehead. "I need to talk to her."

"She's not answering?"

"No."

Aimee hesitates again. "Give her a little time, Andy. She's pissed, yeah, but she's not stupid. She just... needed out."

I exhale sharply, pushing down the frustration. "I need to see her. I'm not waiting too long."

"I didn't think you would," Aimee's voice softens. "I'll let you know if she leaves."

"Thanks."

After we hang up, I stare at my phone, debating whether to call Mason again. Whether to say something, anything, so she knows she's not alone.

But I already know how that'll go. She won't pick up.

And then there's Alex. I hate that this is happening. I hate that Mason had to fight this fight alone.

But Alex? He must be feeling it, too. He had to take it to Robert and stand there while Mason went head-to-head with Elitus and McGuire. He couldn't stop it.

As much as I want to hate him—for all of it—part of me knows.

He must feel guilty. And the worst part?

Even after everything, the silence, the distance, the wreckage, I still care.

I let my phone drop onto the bed beside me and pull my knees to my chest. I stare at the screen, willing Mason to call.

Willing Alex to find me.

But they don't.

TEN

Alex

I stop by Dad's, but Mason won't see me. I barely get a word out before Mom and Mama tear into me. Aimee joins in, sharp with disappointment, and even Mya doesn't hold back.

The only person deeper in the doghouse is Dad. Max doesn't say much, just that I need to talk to Mason, and bringing chocolate wouldn't hurt. RJ gives me a look so disapproving it stings. Kennedy won't even look at me.

Feeling like a total ass, I retreat to the dorms.

But the tension follows me like a storm cloud.

The gossip's already spread, just as I expected. Most of them already fear Mason, and now? Now they think she might turn.

It's not true. But there's a wall between her and the rest of them, and it's only getting taller.

They fear her power, but they don't know her. She'd die for most of them—no hesitation. But that's not what they see. They see the weapon McGuire is turning her into.

In the common area, I see the last person I know will give me hell. Andy.

She's curled in a chair, legs tucked under her, reading some romance novel she'll deny later. I drop into the chair across from her.

She knows I'm here but doesn't acknowledge it.

I deserve it. I don't even know what I'm supposed to say. She pushed me on purpose last night. Part of it; frustration over our situation. But the other part? She's disappointed in me.

Somehow, that stings more than my parents' disappointment ever could.

The more distance I try to put between us, the harder it gets.

My feelings for her keep growing.

I hate the distance, but being near her? That's almost worse.

Andy

I hear him coming before I see him—heavy steps, a sigh, guilt clinging to him like a storm cloud.

Alex drops into the chair across from me. I pretend not to notice, eyes glued to the book in my lap. I don't even pay attention to what I am reading. It doesn't matter. He's here, and he knows damn well I'm ignoring him.

"Andy."

I flip a page I haven't read.

"I'm sorry."

I don't look up. "It's not me you need to apologize to."

"I tried with Mase. She's mad; she has every right to be. But that doesn't mean she's the only one I owe an apology to."

My fingers tighten around the book, frustration spiking hot in my chest. With a sharp snap, I shut it and stand.

If he wants to talk, we're going somewhere private. I may worry and still care, but that doesn't mean I will censor my opinion of the situation.

I don't check to see if he's following. I already know he is.

Leaving the suite door open, I head into my room, not bothering to check if Roarke's back. The second Alex steps inside, I round on him.

"What do you want me to say, Alex? You should've known backing McGuire would set her off. All she ever wants is for someone to say, 'Good job' Is that so freaking hard?"

Alex rolls his eyes. "Trust me, everyone is well aware of how superior she is."

"But does she know that?" I snap, "She needs someone to tell her that. To change how she sees herself. I hate that you don't see what is happening. Or choose to do anything about it. You and Roarke both. We're your sisters!"

"Roarke is proud of you. I'm proud of you. And of her. You two are some of the most important Threes we have," Alex says.

"Being important to the mission isn't what she's looking for! That's like being needed at your job. What she wants is for her brother to show her she matters more than the mission. Just because we are women doesn't mean we are less!"

He exhales, rubbing a hand down his face. He gets it, but he won't say it. Alex has always had a tough time admitting he's mistaken.

But he's trying. And I hate how much that still matters to me.

"She's not just a soldier, Alex. Neither am I," my voice softens. "You say we're more than mission operatives...but does it feel that way? Because to me? To her? It doesn't."

His jaw tightens. He sees it now, the exhaustion in me, the weight of being needed but never valued beyond our abilities. "Andy—"

"No. You listen." I step closer, my fists clenched. "You get to be Alex. Riddick gets to be Riddick. Kyle gets to be Kyle. But Mason and me? We're weapons. That's all everyone sees."

"We get sent out. We get pushed harder. Expected to do more. And when we push back—when we ask for anything outside of this—we're labeled unstable. Reckless. A risk. Treated like we can't take care of ourselves, that we need protection or to be controlled."

The anger in my chest burns hot, but beneath it, is something deeper. Something I can't say aloud. Years of being treated like an asset first, a person second.

"So yeah, Mason blew up. And you all watched. You all let it happen. And now she's locked away, while McGuire figures out what to do with her and when it's over?" I pause, letting it all sink in. "It'll just start again."

Alex's shoulders drop, and he exhales slowly, nodding. "I'll try to do better," he says. "When she talks to me. In the meantime, I owe you an apology. I shouldn't have snapped at you last night. You were supporting her. And even though I don't like how it all played out...I pushed her there."

"It's fine, Alex."

"It's not fine, Andy," he says, stepping closer. "I should've controlled my temper. Taking it out on you is never okay."

"Apology accepted. I get it. I may have meant to rile you up," I say, offering a small smile.

His relief is immediate, and it tightens something in my chest. He doesn't think he deserves forgiveness, and maybe he doesn't.

But I'm forgiving him, anyway. Because no matter how pissed I get, he still matters to me. I place a tentative hand on his arm. "She'll forgive you, just like I am. Give her some time."

"I will," he gives me a soft smile. "Andy, I mean it. Thank you. And I know I don't say it enough, but you, Mason—all of you—you're more than just mission operatives. I hope you know that."

I look away, swallowing the lump in my throat. Alex tips my chin up, and our eyes meet—his gaze softer than I expect.

"Thank you," I whisper.

Before he can stop me, I melt into him, wrapping my arms around his waist as he presses a kiss to my forehead.

I know I shouldn't forgive him this quickly.

But when he looks at me like this, holds me like this, it's hard to remember why I was mad at all. I stay in his embrace, letting it sink into my bones.

The door swings open, and Roarke steps inside.

I don't let go. Neither does Alex.

Roarke doesn't look shocked, just amused, like he expected this.

"You two done being dramatic?" he drawls.

I smirk and step back, nudging Alex as I do. "Maybe. Depends on whether Alex plans to do something stupid again."

Roarke snorts. "Odds aren't great."

"Hey," Alex mutters, but there's no bite to it.

I roll my eyes. "How was your mission?"

Roarke shrugs, dropping into the chair by my desk. "Charley was in a mood."

That means Roarke let Charley take her frustrations out on him—and he didn't bother to heal.

Like Alex, wanting the pain to make something about the situation feel better.

"You deserve it," I tell him, only half-serious. He flashes a crooked grin.

"How's Mason?" he asks as Alex takes a seat on my bed.

"Locked away at home. Probably plotting Elitus' demise with Wyatt," Alex says.

Roarke smirks. Those two hate Elitus more than anyone else.

Wyatt's the teacher, and Mason's biggest supporter of her academic abilities. Even though he's an X-One, Wyatt hates combat and refuses to fight for McGuire.

Instead, he throws everything into teaching, training, and developing the rest.

For the first time today, the air in the room feels a little lighter. Roarke lounges comfortably, and Alex looks more relaxed than I've seen him in days.

This is what I miss. Fewer missions, more friendship. We are like a family sometimes, but it gets lost in mission rosters and training.

For tonight, I will let myself enjoy it, even if it's only temporary.

Eleven

Andy

For the last couple of weeks, it's been... calm.

April passed in a blur. The tournament went on without Mason. It wasn't the same.

Alex and I have reached a truce, more than before, but still not enough. Roarke plays dumb, but I'm fairly sure he knows how I feel about Alex, and how much it messes with me. He suspects but says nothing.

Alex is still Alex; polite, nice, and sweet when he wants to be, but always following Elitus' rules. He keeps his distance most of the time. But I see him trying.

He's more sociable, showing up more than he used to.

With Mason stuck at home, there aren't any actual parties.

But we still hang out, have movie nights, and spend lazy evenings lingering in common spaces with friends.

It's almost normal. Almost.

It's been tense for the combatants. Without Mason in the lineup, the workload has shifted, and training is nowhere near as fun.

The gossip is stale without her feeding me the latest information, and as much as I hate to admit it, I miss her. I didn't realize how much everything revolved around her until she was gone.

She's also one of the few I can talk to about Alex. Who gets what it's like to want something you might never have.

She makes me hold on a little longer. She believes in fate, and sometimes... she makes a believer out of me, too.

I visit her, of course. But I'm not the only one. There's a steady stream of visitors in and out of her house. Notably absent, though? Riddick. Kyle. Roarke. Her combat partners.

I called Roarke out on it. But he's focused on training. Not just himself but helping Mya and RJ more. With Mason out, he took on Mya as a personal student. She is sixteen and already kicking serious ass. And unlike when she is with Kyle, she listens to Roarke.

I appreciate him taking the time because Mya needs it. She appears tough, but inside, she is soft. She battles as hard as Mason and loves the combat role.

But sometimes I wonder, is it what she wants? Or just something she does because of her lineage.

Mya is the only Gen Four in the dorms; she is gearing up for full combat. She does minor missions but hasn't led a full squad yet. Sometimes, she makes Mason look lazy. Being super focused on combat and technique, she's an expert with weapons and is tracking as a High Tier Three Spectrum. Her roommate and cousin, Siobhan, another female spectrum, has been working with her on Tier Twos. They work well together and make a solid team.

Mason, for her part, is losing her mind from boredom. The only upside? She's finally finished a lot of her coursework.

As a Three, we learn fast. As a One and a Three? Mason is on another level. Photographic memory, instant recall—she has a Rolodex in her brain.

Me? I never cared much for school. But Mason and Wyatt are in an unofficial competition to see who can complete the most degrees.

She's also been spending a lot of time with Kennedy and Maria, which makes her mom happy. When I dropped by the other day, Maria and Joanne were both there, along with Mason's sisters, Aimee, Mya, and little Kennedy.

Joanne took an interest in getting to know me, which was unexpected. Mason smirked through most of the afternoon, so I'm convinced I was set up.

I know Riddick, Roarke, and the rest still go off campus, no matter what's said.

"Boys will be boys," someone commented. It's bullshit. Mason and I could port and leave. Mya too.

But we don't; because it's not worth the fallout. Even if it sucks. I hate thinking about it, but I do.

What happens when I graduate?

Because right now, it's lonely as hell. I spend time with Roarke's crew and with our friends. But no matter how much more I want with Alex, I don't think he will ever break the rules.

He's probably the only one who could convince Elitus to change the rules.

But I doubt he ever will.

Maybe Kyle could. But he'd need dirt on McGuire, and he's so far up his ass, I doubt if Kyle had it, he would use it. Knowing Kyle, if he had it, he would've played that card already—to impress a girl.

Kyle used to battle and spar with Mason all the time. They were close. But after she turned fourteen? It stopped. I don't know why. He still flirts with her, works with her, and gives her a tough time. But she told me once—overnight it all changed. Almost as if he realized she wasn't what he wanted. Or maybe... couldn't have.

I know the feeling. Sometimes I wonder if Alex looks at me the same way—like he decided a long time ago that I'm off-limits.

It doesn't matter what I want.

Like tonight, he came through, stopping to talk with Charley, Marty, Kyle, and Nala, then smiled at me before heading out.

That was it.

But it was enough to make me think about him, enough to make it hurt a little more.

I wish I could walk up to him and ask what his deal is. Maybe he'd be honest. I could get an answer. Maybe I could live with it.

But what if he isn't interested anymore? Where does that leave me?

Will he find a commoner to marry? Bring her on campus like it's no big deal.

My parents were commoners. Dad was military-based and recruited into Elitus. Mom evaluated as a candidate for treatments and X. My dad took a job on campus, and they've been here ever since.

Four X kids later, and they will never leave.

Is that what will happen to us?

Part of me wonders why McGuire and the others don't push us together as a science experiment. Supposedly, that's what's happening in the PPG.

There's no confirmation, but whispers say Coral, PPG's only X-level Wight, is pregnant. By Nikolai, Mya's brother.

If that's true—and that baby becomes a weapon for Dmitri—then forget Latents.

That'll be Elitus' next project.

No doubt about it.

TWELVE

Andy

I took a couple of days to recover from the power burn.

Roarke is pissy, blaming himself for letting me go on the mission.

Mason blames herself for not being there instead.

Alex blames himself for not being my shadow.

The only person I blame is McGuire.

Mason's response is to throw herself into intense training. I doubt she even sleeps. She's out of the dorms before anyone else and back after everyone has gone to bed.

It's more than just making up for lost time. Something else has caused this shift.

I can see the exhaustion weighing on her again, and I don't like it.

And on top of that? Alex has been distant again. I hate it. Whatever I thought we had been building; it's slipping away again.

I know he's been busy. Word is that missions have been going sideways: leaked details, shitty intel. No surprises there. For all the wheeling and dealing McGuire does, he can't seem to handle Dmitri and the PPG. They're always lurking.

I'm supposed to run a mission tonight, two weeks after the incident. But Roarke tells me I'm off. He's going instead. I confront him and ask if he did something.

His quote, "I didn't, no."

Which tells me someone else did. And I suspect who. Alex.

My blood boils. Who the hell does he think he is?

I hit the dorms just in time to see Roarke leaving with Mason, Charley, and Riddick.

Alex should be back by now; he was at the gym and off-site with McGuire.

I don't bother knocking. I push his door open. "What the fuck, Alex?"

He's not alone. Max and Jared are with him. I level them both with a glare, a silent get-the-fuck out.

They glance at Alex, then at me. Jared smirks, and Max squeezes my arm as they leave.

"Andy—" Alex starts, but I cut him off.

"I didn't ask you to interfere in my missions. I am a valuable member of the team!"

"I know you are, but this one doesn't require you. Roarke can manage it, especially with Mason and the others. McGuire is being cautious with the coverage."

"I don't give a flying fuck. They slated me, and you had me removed!"

"Roarke and I—"

"Roarke isn't my keeper, either. Neither of you are. How dare you not at least consult with me?"

"Andy, I was just trying—"

"Trying to do what? Control my life? You can't control Mason, so you settle for me instead? Is that it?"

"No, of course not. I want you safe."

"Are you saying I can't take care of myself?"

"No, that's not what I mean."

"It sure as hell sounds like what you mean. If I'm off campus, I'm not safe without an escort. If I'm on missions, I'm not safe either—a liability."

"You're not a liability."

"Then what am I? Because you just told everyone I'm replaceable."

He doesn't answer, not fast enough, not with anything real.

That's when it hits me; he thinks he is protecting me. But he's crippling me.

"Andy—"

"Save it, Alex. This is exactly what I meant weeks ago. With Mason. With all of it. You jackasses don't get it."

I step closer, my voice sharp and heated.

"I may not love missions, but I love having a purpose. I'm useless otherwise. I don't want to be sitting in a lab like my sister. I want to help!"

"You help—I just don't want you in danger."

"Missions, regardless of the situation, are all dangerous. So is training. And driving a car, which—by the way—I'm also not allowed to do off campus. Shopping, you name it!"

"Andy, come on. You want me to say that it's fair? That I think it's right? No, I don't. But I also don't want you out there unless you need to be."

"But it's okay for you to go out there? I don't like it when you run missions. Or Roarke. Or Mason. Or Charley. But guess what, Alex? It's our fucking job."

"It doesn't have to be," he mutters.

He doesn't get it. Shaking my head, I exhale. "Alex, you either need to let me live my life the way I want, without interference, or you need to walk away. Because I am so done with egotistical jackass men telling me what I can and can't do just because I'm a woman."

"Andy, I care about you. I'm only trying—"

"To control me," I cut him off. "You don't ask my opinion. You dictate what you think is best. If I wanted a daddy telling me what to do, I'd move home."

"Andy—"

"Save it, Alex." My voice is bitter, final. "I'm walking away right now, heading out to see them off. I'd love to override your bullshit and send myself back out, but seeing as though my opinion means jack shit to anyone, I'll just go support my friends."

I slam his door extra hard on my way out. I don't bother walking to the labs; I port straight to the hallway outside the war room.

Inside, they're almost ready to depart. Roarke clocks the look on my face and steers clear, but Mason attempts to send me calming vibes. I shove them off.

She and I have talked more about Alex. She saw how he had avoided me. I told her about our time together when she was gone—how it felt different.

Real, like maybe we weren't circling something impossible.

But after the failed mission? He's distant again. Pulled back and shut down, like he always does when he feels too much.

She said she was going to talk to him about me. About us.

But I don't see the point. He'll never give up control.

Never break the rules. Never work to change them, not really.

And I won't let him dictate my missions or life.

I've seen what that kind of control does. I've watched my father do it with my mother for years until she didn't even recognize herself anymore.

It's suffocating.

And I won't live like that.

...But sometimes I wonder.

If we were together, a couple, would it feel different?

Would I mind so much if he wanted a say in where I went, what risks I took, if I knew it came from love and not power?

Maybe I'd let him have a say. But only if he was standing beside me, not above me.

Because I can't be with someone who wants to protect me by holding me back.

But I might fight beside someone who wants to protect me by showing up.

But I guess I'll never know.

THIRTEEN

Alex

I wish I could say I groveled, apologized, and won Andy back.

But I didn't.

What I did was make sure she was safe, even if it meant pissing her off. Maybe that makes me a bastard.

But I'd rather have her safe and hate me than watch her fall in the field because I didn't do enough.

Her Tier Three skills and ability to port can get her out of most messes. What won't save her is that damn selfless streak.

Andy doesn't leave people behind. Especially not Roarke or her friends, and that terrifies me.

I know what she wants; to be included, to stand beside the rest of us like an equal.

She already is. But knowing that doesn't stop the fear.

I watch her slip further away every time she steps into the field for a mission. And I don't know how to hold on without pushing her away even more.

She doesn't understand. I can't say the words. I can't explain how I'm counting down the seconds until she returns. Every time she ports out, I hold my breath. It's not that I don't believe in her; it's that I don't know how to exist in a world where she isn't in it.

I exhale hard as I head to the dorms. I have been avoiding them more than I should, spending most of my time at home with Kennedy or buried in contracts and enhancement proposals at the office.

But today, the dorms are open.

Not for a mission briefing or training, it's a party. Not the kind we used to throw. No alcohol. No chaos. A backyard bash in late July, all to celebrate the Gen Four birthdays.

Kate went all out, planning with her usual flare. Red, white, and blue cover every surface.

The Gen Four birthdays spread from late June to early August—Mya is the oldest, and Zack, Riddick's brother, is the youngest.

I walk in and the place is overflowing. Even Gen Fives are here. With no parents in sight, only Wights. All the generations, ranging in age from myself, at almost twenty-two, to the youngest wights, Gen Five, who are only eleven. It's a different vibe today. Calm, but more somber than a birthday party should be.

Looking around the common area, I spot Mason leaning against the bar, a bottle of water in front of her. She is entertaining Kennedy, who sits on a stool. Kennedy has a Shirley Temple and a grin so wide it's glowing.

Mason's smiling, too. A real one. It's the first time she's relaxed in weeks. She's been a machine. If she's not giving me shit about Andy, she's drilling everyone with shielding techniques. She's submitted more lessons and training sessions to Elitus than I can count, because she never stops working.

Everyone's noticed. She made up for her month-long sabbatical in no time. She maxes out every test, fights daily in the arena, and pushes herself to exhaustion.

Her power levels are off the charts. Standing near her gives me a surge, like a current running under my skin.

It's impressive. It's also terrifying. No matter how often we talk to her; Bastian, me, even our parents. She won't slow down.

It's been almost three months since her return, and she's only sped up.

I've learned my lesson with Andy. I'm not going to McGuire again.

He's thrilled that Mason has become the weapon he's always wanted. But Riddick's been more agitated than usual. He feels responsible for it.

Mason still trains with the guys, but she has focused on the younger female wights—especially Mya and Siobhan.

They're strong. She's making sure they're ready for whatever's coming.

But socially? Mason is absent. No parties. No drinking. The dorms miss her wild side.

I do, too. Back when she let herself cut loose, Andy did as well. She laughed more. She looked at me as if maybe we could be something.

Now, Andy barely looks at me at all. I know I deserve it and just need to get used to it. But it's hard most days, and even with distance, it isn't getting easier. If anything, it's getting harder.

I hope today gives everyone a break—just one day without missions, intel briefings, or fallout. One day when we get to remember, we're still human.

Andy

I bring Ava and De over to the party. Roarke was training with Mya this morning. Unfortunately, my father was at home. He ignored me as usual and didn't even bother to say hi. My mother, the eternal doormat, stayed silent and only whispered to my sisters. She didn't even look at me. She never does when he's around. I used to think she was afraid of him, that she was trying to mitigate the risk. Now? I think she just gave up; on him, me, everything.

I grab their stuff. They're both sleeping over somewhere tonight, something that's become routine. Rina, Riddick's sister, is one of Ava's best friends. And De and Aimee are inseparable.

The dorms are overflowing. No alcohol today, at least not out in the open. Mya and RJ are combat-enabled Gen Fours, and Mya is the only one who lives in the dorms, much to the frustration of my sister and her friends. Delilah, Aimee, Hope, and her gaggle wish they could leave home. But they're stuck.

There's been talks behind closed doors, murmurs about building condos or town-homes for the non-combat Gens. They're turning seventeen, old enough to want and plan for independence, even if they're not in the field. Old enough to see the double standard.

I'm thankful Roarke got us out early and into the dorms at age ten. I went full combat to make it happen. Scars, bruises, endless training, it didn't matter. I was getting out.

Behind me, the bass from the party thumps through the floorboards. Laughter and shouting echo down the hallway, summer heat clinging to everything.

Around the back, I spot Mason, who is sitting on the edge of the pool. She looks incredible. All that nonstop training has toned her already killer body even more. She is in a modest two-piece, well compared to Charley's minuscule bikini. Mason is in bright blue—matching her eyes when they aren't glowing that signature X-level violet. Mason's hair is up in a high ponytail, her skin lighter than usual, but that's because of her never-ending training and skipping the pool days.

Charley, Mason, and RJ toss pool toys for Kennedy and Elijah, Nick Thompson's youngest son. They are both five years old and start classes in the fall.

I slip off my cover-up. I don't have the curves those two are flaunting, but it's not nothing—or so De likes to reassure me. My tankini is yellow, my favorite color. I join them, dunking my feet into the pool.

It's an Olympic-sized pool that is overflowing with bodies and noise today. The side porches, back lawn, people are everywhere.

Kate waves at me. I helped her with some of the setup this morning. We rarely have events like this, but even Kate, who is not a partier, knew we needed this.

Lately, it's been too quiet, too tense. Everyone is on edge, nerves shot. It's like we're all waiting for something to go wrong.

Alex stands with Kyle, Bastian, and Max, deep in conversation. He looks good; board shorts, an unbuttoned Hawaiian shirt, and aviators hiding his eyes.

He never misses a gym session with Roarke and Riddick, so I'm not surprised. Those three are gym rats worshiping at the altar of Nate Ames—Kate's dad, our trainer, and part-time comedian.

Roarke joins them not long after, fresh from a shower. A few light bruises dot his chest, but they'll be gone by midafternoon. Mya's with him, and she's glowing. Her dark hair is freshly cut into a sleek bob; sunglasses perched on her face like armor.

She shoves Max as she passes. He catches himself before toppling into the water and shoots her a look that promises payback.

Mya slips off her sundress, revealing a black bikini that makes me feel like I'm wearing a tent. Charley whistles, and Mya answers with a small, amused smile. "Wow," Charley laughs. "Mason looks like I got a new partner in the hot girl club."

Mya shakes her head, but Mason smiles at them both.

"Today is testing a few guys' limits," Aimee says, swimming up. "Maybe some will finally grow a pair and break the rules." Delilah, Siobhan, and Hope trail behind her. De hands Mya a cup of spiked lemonade. I guess the birthday crew is drinking after all.

"If I lived in the dorms, those rules would've been toast years ago," Hope says, grinning. Siobhan shoots her younger sister with a glare.

"What?" Hope shrugs. "Just because you all follow Elitus' dumbass rules doesn't mean we have to. One more year, and what can they do? Pull us from combat?" De, Aimee, and Hope exchange matching smiles, laughing.

Well... there's that. They're not in combat. There's not much Elitus can hold over them. I wish I had that kind of freedom.

My eyes drift to Alex. He's mid-conversation, but I can almost feel his gaze on me. Things have been distant between us. He's been avoiding the dorms, avoiding me.

I'm still off missions, and yeah, it pisses me off.

But even if he hadn't blocked me, I wouldn't be assigned to any missions. Mason has been taking on double the load. Mya is stepping up, leaving little left for me.

It makes me wonder what that means for my future. Graduation's not far away, and I still don't know what comes next, especially if I'm not in combat. I hate the lab, and I'm awful at teaching. And the worst part? I don't see where else I fit. It's frustrating as hell.

But in my mind, I already know what I want, what I've always wanted.

Before I spiral too far, a little voice and a pair of wet hands smack against my knees.

"Come get a snack with me."

I look down at Kennedy. Her light blue eyes, the same color as Alex's, make my heart ache.

I nod, lean down, and pull her out of the pool. We walk together, hand in hand, and head to the food table. She babbles nonstop about what she got her three siblings for their birthdays, filling me in on all the latest Clarke Family drama.

She's a weird mash-up of Aimee, Mya, and Mason—all energy, sass, and secrets. We sit and chat, and Kennedy eats her body weight in snacks. I look up to see Alex heading our way.

Kennedy jumps up to hug him, soaking his shirt. He laughs and steals a cookie off her plate. He takes a seat across from me and smiles. I love it—and hate it.

See. That's the problem.

The only thing I want... is him.

FOURTEEN

Alex

Summer winds down, and my focus is on contracts and restructuring—working with Kate to create opportunities for Gen Twos, who aren't combat-classified, without damaging morale or compromising our future.

Most have been training to do lab, classroom, or office work.

Andy finished her schooling and spent the summer in the lab doing admin work. It kept her busy. Bored out of her mind, but busy.

The distance continues to grow between Andy and me. I know it's my fault, but I don't know if I can fix it.

And it's not just affecting things with Andy. It's bleeding into everything, including her brother.

Roarke's been pulling away, not just from me, but from everyone. Even Riddick's noticed. He keeps his head down, buried in training or locked in the gym, pushing harder than usual. Sparring with anyone who'll take him on.

When he's not training, he's off campus for hours, coming back exhausted, but unreadable.

I've noticed he avoids certain people, Mya especially.

Something happened between them. They were fine at the party, but after that. Everything shifted.

Whatever happened, it changed them. He was her advocate, her regular partner, her primary trainer.

Now, Roarke's harder. Colder.

Mya? She's more focused than ever, not just because she's preparing for full combat. She's running from something.

I try to bring it up, but Mya won't talk. Mason has noticed too. She gets brushed off as well. You don't push Mya. If you do, she will shut you out.

But I don't like it. I don't enjoy watching them become a version of themselves no one recognizes.

Roarke may be one of my closest friends, but the distance between us feels like too much. I know he's staying away, buried in missions, drowning in pressure.

Missions, training, graduation prep, drama with his parents and sisters, and his constant need to disappear, it's impossible to pin Roarke down.

But today, I catch him in his room. "You got a minute?" I ask, tapping the door as I step inside.

He's tying his sneakers, half-dressed; like he's getting ready to disappear again.

"I have a minute," he says, not looking up.

"I want to apologize."

That gets his attention. He glances up, brow furrowing. Not defensive, just cautious. "For what?"

"For Andy. Or whatever's made you avoid me."

Roarke stands up. He's not the tallest guy, just over six feet, but he's broad. Built. Only Riddick tops him in bulk. Strength and grit keep him on the front lines, even though he hates it almost as much as Wyatt, Max, and RJ.

"So, you're finally admitting something happened with my twin?" he asks, judgment flashing in his eyes.

"Something?" I scoff. "I don't know what you think happened, but it wasn't much. I won't lie—I care about her. I know I've been all over the place and probably caused her some heartache. That was never my intention. I just wanted her safe."

"I know you went to McGuire to get her pulled from missions," he says, shrugging into his jacket. "I don't care about that. She doesn't need to be out there—never has. Let her be mad. If I had the power, I would've done it years ago. I'm mad you didn't have the guts to come to me and say you're in love with her."

"I—" The words catch in my throat. Love? Shit. Do I love her? Riddick's said it before, but I don't know. I never let myself go there. I couldn't.

I swallow hard and force myself to meet his gaze. "I'm not sure what I am supposed to say to that," I admit.

"You say, 'Sorry, Roarke. I'm a stupid ass, and I'm going to make it up to you and your sister—if she'll forgive me,'" he says, dead serious.

I laugh, but it feels forced. Freaking Roarke, always the peacemaker. He has a way of cutting through the bullshit I try to hide. I take a deep breath, and I realize he's right.

"Sorry, Roarke. I'm in love with your sister. I don't know how to repair what I broke, but I want to try—if she'll even talk to me."

He smirks. "You need to get Elitus to drop the dating ban."

"I know you think I'm a god," I joke, "but even I'm not that powerful."

"Someone's got to," he mutters, frustration creeping in. "You think you're the only one stuck? You're not."

It catches me off guard. I step closer, noticing the tension in his shoulders. He looks like he's holding everything in. Normally, he's the fun one, the pressure valve for the rest of us. Steady. The one that balances out Riddick and Mason. That's why they work so well together. But right now, he looks like he's about to break something, or someone.

"You want to come out and grab a beer?" he asks.

I haven't been off base in weeks, but if it means digging into whatever's eating at him and maybe fixing some of the mess I made, I'm in.

We step into the hallway, and I spot Mya, heading straight toward us.

Roarke stiffens. His entire demeanor shifts; jaw tight, eyes dark. The easy-going mask vanishes, replaced by something cold and sealed shut.

I don't know what happened, but it's changed everything. Mya used to be his exception, the one person outside his sisters who could get past the walls. Now they are both on edge, and not speaking.

"Hey, what's wrong?" I ask. Mya narrows her eyes at Roarke first, sharp, accusatory, then turns them to me.

"Besides Mason being a fucking robot?"

"Well…" I do not know how to respond to that either. I know Mya was supposed to be on a low-risk mission tonight.

"She pushed me off the mission. It seems you're not the only one with a say in assignments."

That's not like Mason. She'd kick my ass if I tried to pull something like that on her or Mya. "Are you sure it was her?"

Mya hesitates, eyes narrowing. Then she glances at Roarke, whose face stays locked in that tight, unreadable mask. And for the first time, I see something in her that isn't fire or fury.

It's a disappointment. Sadness. That's almost worse.

"Not sure, no. But she's out on it. When she gets back? I'll get answers. You can bet your ass on that."

Her tone's sharp, but her eyes stay locked on Roarke, demanding something he won't give. He meets her gaze, but the set of his jaw. His entire body is tight, defensive, like he's bracing for a fight he knows he'll lose.

She crosses her arms, tilting her head. "Where the hell are you two going?"

She says it to both of us, but her eyes are on Roarke.

"Out," he says. "Alex and I are grabbing a beer."

"Really?" she says, voice all venom and edge. "Well, don't let my young, dumb, seventeen-year-old ass keep you."

Her words hit like a slap. She doesn't wait for a response. She spins on her heel and storms back upstairs.

I glance at Roarke. He clenches his jaw and shakes his head.

"Do I even want to know?" I ask.

He doesn't answer, pulls out his keys, and spins them between his fingers.

"You coming or not?"

I nod, dropping a quick text to Riddick, in case I need backup. With the mood Roarke is in, who knows what kind of trouble he will stir up.

Riddick meets us at Route 7, a local dive bar with pool tables, darts, and a loyal college crowd. It's the kind of place we hit when we need to disappear into the noise.

He finds us at a high top in the back, nodding at the server, who already knows to bring our refills and a fresh beer for him.

"How was it?" Roarke asks, leaning back in his chair, half-listening to Riddick, half scanning the bar like he's hunting for a distraction.

"Easy. Mya would've been fine. I don't know why she got pulled. Mason was bored."

"Did Mason pull her?" I ask.

Riddick laughs, shaking his head. "That's what I figured," I mutter.

"No idea who made the call. Mya was pissed. Mason plans to talk to her—and McGuire."

He turns to me. "I know you don't want to hear it, Alex, but she's more than ready for full combat. Both RJ and her. She wants it."

Roarke drains his beer and signals for another, but his silence clings to him.

Something is bothering him, deeper than Mya getting benched. Whether it's her, Andy, Mason... or something else, I can feel the weight of it.

"What's up with you?" Riddick asks, nodding in our direction. "You get your mess sorted out?"

Instead of answering, Roarke smirks, motioning toward me. "Alex is going to figure out how to get Elitus to drop the ban."

"I didn't exactly say that." I mutter. "But I'll bring it up. I know Mom's on my side. Shit, all I need to do is put Sarah, Maria, and Mom on the task, throw in Coach Nate and Nikki for backup."

We exchange a look and laugh, easy and familiar. This is how it's always been. Effortless, even when we don't see eye to eye. The mission stress, training chaos, and Elitus drama all fade when it's just us.

"That's not a horrible idea," Roarke says, his grin spreading. "God knows Coach Nate is always down for a fight with McGuire."

Kate's dad—our coach, trainer, and off-the-record cheerleader. He's been secretly championing our off-base adventures for years, though he'll never admit it to Kate. She might hate Elitus' double standard even more than Mason does.

A group of college girls circles our table, moving like sharks who smell blood. Roarke catches the eye of a blond and smirks, an open invitation. He thrives on attention, using it as a distraction. Riddick and I exchange a look before turning back to each other, letting him do his thing.

"You really planning to get back with Andy?" Riddick asks, voice casual, eyes anything but. "I'm all for it. But Roarke's right. You need to handle Elitus first."

"I'm working on it. I won't go near her until I'm sure I won't have to walk away again. What that means... or how long it'll take? I don't know."

"Wish I had a simple answer. But we both know they'll fight it. Andy is still off missions?"

"Yeah."

"Did you have anything to do with Mya?"

"No. I didn't even know until she confronted us tonight. She was pissed."

"Can't blame her. She's been sidelined for a bit, but Mason will straighten it out. She's seventeen, and the final combat rounds are coming up. No doubt she will fully enable on Threes. Her spectrum range will help push them into allowing it."

Roarke is only half-listening, eyes on the blond now leaning against his chair. Like clockwork, he flirts, he smiles, he disappears.

And we let him.

Riddick and I play a few rounds of darts, keeping the talk light; sports, random crap, anything but Elitus.

Roarke's been gone for a solid half-hour. When he returns, he looks relaxed... but the tension's still there, coiled beneath the surface like always.

By the time we're back through the gates, it's 2 a.m.

The dorms are dead; only a few lights are still on.

Wights need little sleep unless we've burned a lot of power. We head to the main kitchen to get food. Andy's already there waiting to check on her brother.

She barely glances at me. Her mental shields are up, stronger than usual.

Mason's work, no doubt.

"Have a good time?" she asks, her voice unreadable.

"Yep," Roarke mutters, suddenly fascinated by what's inside the fridge.

"Hmm," she murmurs, and somehow it hits harder than a shout.

"Just wanted to make sure you got back in one piece. Night, Riddick."

Andy

I've never been to Route 7.

But I've heard enough stories to know it's a low-light dive tucked off some forgotten stretch of highway. Pool tables with warped legs. Sticky floors. Neon beer signs buzz above a too-loud jukebox. A place that smells of spilled whiskey, sweat, and stale cigarette smoke. College kids love it.

It's where they go to disappear. To be someone else, or no one at all. And tonight, it's where Riddick said Alex and Roarke went.

I told myself I didn't care.

Roarke needs a night off. He's been walking around like a bomb with a cut wire for the last few weeks; tense, moody, avoiding talking and everyone. Even training hasn't helped. He needs a break. He deserves that. I want that for him.

But Alex?

That's different.

Alex Clarke doesn't get to vanish into some shitty bar and act like everything's fine. He doesn't get to laugh, drink, or shoot pool. While I'm stuck here. No missions, and no purpose.

He's been drifting in and out of my life like a ghost for too long; present, but unreachable. He looks like he wants to say something...and then says nothing.

He's waiting for me to forget what it felt like when he pulled me in, kissed me until I didn't know my name, and then pushed me away like I was nothing.

So, no, I'm not thrilled that he went out. And I'm done pretending otherwise.

I'm in the kitchen when they come back. I hear the door—the soft click, the muffled thud of boots on the tile, but I don't turn around, not right away.

I keep organizing the counter, as if the salt and pepper shakers are my top priority.

Roarke comes in first, jacket slung over one shoulder, hair tousled. He looks relaxed, not like he's carrying the world on his shoulders. He mumbles something about being hungry and heads for the fridge.

Then he walks in. Alex. Dark jeans, sleeves pushed up, shirt collar rumpled like someone brushed against him too many times.

He looks relaxed. And that pisses me off.

He doesn't even say anything, pauses in the doorway. I don't acknowledge him. I refuse.

He doesn't get to leave me on read in real life, vanish for hours without a word, and then show up like it is business as usual.

I raise my shields like Mason taught me—slow, intentional, cold.

I know he feels it. The wall I've built. The difference between the girl who used to light up around him...and the one who doesn't even look his way.

"Have a good time?" I ask, voice casual, even.

Roarke grunts, still digging through leftovers. "Yeah."

"Hmm."

I turn away. "Just wanted to make sure you got back in one piece. Night, Riddick."

Not Alex. I don't look at him; I won't say his name.

I feel his gaze following me, heat crawling down my spine. But I keep walking. Every step is a little more forced than the last.

I slip into my room, closing the door behind me like I can shut the night out.

Silence presses in—heavier than it should be. I lean back against the door, eyes closed, trying to shake the bitter mix of irritation, longing and something far more dangerous clawing at my chest.

It's time I moved on.

Get over it. It won't change; it's only making me more miserable.

I have a few weeks before I graduate.

Maybe after that, I can figure out the future. One that isn't just a "combat weapon".

I have to try. Hoping for a future with Alex?

That's never going to happen.

Alex

Riddick is silently laughing, barely holding it together. Roarke doesn't even bother hiding his smirk.

After Andy's gone, they both burst out laughing at my expense.

"Ah, man, I almost feel bad," Roarke says. "She has a mean temper. And she loves fucking with you."

"One of these days, you'll meet your match too, Roarke."

His smirk falters—just for a second. "Not likely. Bachelor for life over here."

Riddick snorts, shaking his head. "Yeah, sure. Let's see how that fantasy holds up."

We all know Roarke's been off. Buried in distractions, training, anything to avoid whatever's eating at him.

But we don't push.

Not yet.

That's the thing about the three of us—we call each other out, but only when we know it'll land.

And Roarke?

He's not there yet.

FIFTEEN

Alex

I'm pacing. Not physically, just in my head. The same loop circling until it's carved into my skull.

I'm plotting, strategizing, cycling through possibilities I've already ruled out a dozen times. This isn't abstract anymore.

It's personal. Close. Too damn close.

I lean forward at my desk, elbows braced against a stack of policy drafts and confidential memos I'm not even supposed to have, but that's never stopped me. The desk lamp throws a low light across my notes. The laptop hums softly. A half-full coffee cup sits by my elbow, going cold. I've read the same paragraph on inter-departmental relational clauses three times now, and none of it means shit.

Because Elitus controls everything.

Our training.

Assignments.

Living quarters.

Relationships.

Our future.

As much as I love my moms, I trust them to fight for us, but I know the truth: they're not the ones calling the shots. Not really. McGuire and the board have their claws in everything. The system was built to keep us controlled emotionally and physically.

We're not supposed to pair off, not without approval. We're not meant to choose each other. Not when Elitus has already chosen our paths for us.

With Gen Two's birthdays and graduation approaching fast, the pressure's building. I can feel it in every mission and briefing. The decisions made about our roles and placements will shape the rest of our lives.

That should terrify me.

But what scares me?

That I'm too late. Too late to save whatever is between Andy and me.

I hate admitting it. But it's there, gnawing at me like rot beneath the surface. The longer I am unable to change things, the more the space between us stretches into something I might never cross.

My frustration bubbles up, making it impossible to think. My chest feels tight. My jaw aches from clenching. I glance down at my phone for the fiftieth time tonight.

Nothing. No message. No missed calls. Just that empty screen reminds me of what I've lost, what I could've had and walked away from.

The worst part?

I don't want to play games. Not with her. Not with this. But I know I have been.

I don't want to pretend that I'm indifferent. I don't want to act like I'm okay with her moving on, because I'm not.

But wanting her and having her? That's where everything falls apart.

Until I find a way to protect her, I can't ask her to risk everything. Not when I'm not sure what I'm risking.

And still...

What if, by the time I figure it out, she's already done waiting?

What if she gives that fire to someone else?

Someone without all this responsibility.

Someone who can walk into a room and pull her close—without wondering if the walls have ears.

The thought cuts deeper than I want to admit. I press my palms into my eyes, breathing deep, trying to quiet the spiral. But the questions keep coming; louder, sharper, harder to ignore.

How do I fight a system that was built to keep us apart?

How do I choose her without burning down everything else I've built?

I don't know. And for the first time in a long time... I hate how much that answer scares me.

After dinner with Max, I head back to the dorms. Late summer heat still clings to the air. My birthday is next week, and not long after that, Gen Two's graduation is in late October.

The place is quieter than usual. Mason mentioned she was going overseas for a shopping trip; I do not know how she convinced Kyle to take her.

I'm just glad she went. "Robot Mason" taking a backseat for once. She's a machine for McGuire, an Elitus prototype. But at least she's looking forward to fall and graduation for Gen Twos.

Even though the idea of her being off base makes me nervous, I know Kyle will look out for her. I'm assuming Charley is going too.

The only time Mason relaxes is when it's about her girls. She has a soft spot for Andy, Charley, Marty, and even Siobhan. Our sisters, Kennedy and Aimee, get past her walls. But it's Mya, her battle partner, that keeps her grounded the most. She helps balance friendship, family, and the relentless grind.

I step onto the balcony and spot her with Bastian and a few others, their laughter drifting into the warm night air. Kyle, as usual, is being himself—flirting, flashing that damn grin that always seems to work for him. I shake my head, relieved the grin isn't aimed at Mason, and turn away.

Then, out of the corner of my eye, I see it, a familiar flash of blond in Kyle's arms.

What the...

No fucking way.

Andy

After a much-needed day away from the dorm drama, we head back, calm energy still lingering between us. Bastian and Mason tucked into a corner, sharing a drink and deep in conversation. Kyle's been surprisingly attentive. He's a flirt, almost as bad as my brother, but tonight, his sole focus is on me.

I'm sure the reason for the attention is that Mason has been so focused on Bastian. He has never shown an interest in me, as anything more than a fellow Tier Three.

Kyle and Mason were once close, and Mason used to have a big crush on him. But sometime around when missions started up, he started ignoring her. She went from being his sidekick to the afterthought. I know it hurt her, and although she never spoke about it, it has jaded her towards guys and relationships.

Maybe he is trying to make her jealous, or maybe I am the distraction to keep him from being jealous. Either way, I'll take it.

It's been a while since I've felt like the center of anyone's attention. Today has been good. It has done a decent job of taking my mind off other things. It's nice just to relax with friends. I've been bored, and going off base with them has been a pleasant change of pace.

Part of me is still bitter about being sidelined from combat. I don't even know what comes after graduation, and Roarke is not helping—just playing jackass big brother, telling me to be thankful that I'm off the mission roster, like I haven't trained for this my whole life.

I weigh my options, frustrated. But flirting with Kyle? That would serve Alex right.

Kyle hasn't let up, even back at the dorms. He's been attentive, his hand brushing mine, eyes holding longer than they should. It's all choreographed, all perfectly played. And don't get me wrong, I have heard the stories about when Kyle has been off base with the others. But that he is like this with me? In public, at the dorms? It makes me wonder about his purpose. It also makes me aggravated.

Alex won't even sit with me in public, and Kyle, well, he is coming on strong. When I turn to him to tell him it's been fun, but no thanks, he steps closer to me. Really close. Putting his arm around my back, pulling me into him. I take a deep breath, thinking of a way to explain that I can't go there with him, but I don't get a chance.

There is a blur of motion. Kyle is ripped away from me and punched in the face.

I expect it to be Roarke, ever the protector. But I'm mistaken.

It's Alex.

Kyle rights himself, cursing. The room shifts; the calm energy is gone, replaced with raw tension.

"What the hell is wrong with you, Alex?" I shout, stepping between them before Kyle can retaliate.

"What's wrong with me? What's wrong with you?" Alex is fuming, eyes blazing. His whole body is tight, fists clenched. "Jesus Christ, Andy. He had his hands all over you!"

"And I liked it." The words are out before I can stop them.

Sharp. Defiant. A challenge.

Alex's resolve snaps. His power surges; crackling, alive. Mason is on it instantly, stepping between us, hands raised.

The charge in the room is suffocating, a storm brewing beneath Alex's skin.

Kyle is pissed, but he doesn't push it. Alex is already on the verge of losing it completely, his whole body vibrating with rage.

Weaponized. With his powers emerging, an eerie metallic sheen crawls across his skin.

And then Kyle, the idiot, makes a comment about me being single.

Damn it.

Alex spins faster than I can track and swings at Kyle. But Mason steps in between, trying to stop it, and she takes the impact. She jerks back, gasps, as blood blossoms across her ribcage, a vivid contrast against her white shirt.

Everything stops.

The world narrows into a single, horrifying moment.

"Shit," Roarke curses, appearing just in time to catch Mason before she collapses. Bastian is at her side, his face tight with panic.

Chaos erupts around us.

Kyle is yelling at Alex. Riddick storms in, demanding answers.

Alex stands there frozen. Staring at his own hands like they don't belong to him.

And me? I can't move. I can't think. Mason is bleeding. Tears sting my eyes, my chest tightens—guilt, rage, all of it crashing in.

This is my fault.

If I hadn't...

If I'd just...

Bailey rushes in, and Mason insists he take her to his parents, so Reese and Nala can work on her, avoiding the infirmary. She doesn't want Alex to get into trouble. She'll be fine, eventually. But still.

Bastian frowns, holding her hand, his energy pulsing out toward her. Trying to heal her, but she tells him to stay and deal with Kyle.

I follow behind once I'm calm enough to port.

When I arrive, Reese is finishing up her healing.

"I'm so sorry," I tell Mason. She's healing, but it's slow. Instead of focusing on herself, she's trying to untangle me.

My emotions are a wreck; one more thing she's trying to fix.

"You don't need to be sorry. Just don't be stupid, okay? Starting a war with Alex won't get you anywhere," Mason says softly.

I bite my tongue, trying to shove the hurt from my eyes—somewhere less visible.

"I know. He just... gets under my skin. I lose it. Shit flies out of my mouth. It's bad. He's pissed. Hurt. We're done for good this time. I saw his face. He would've killed Kyle. But it's worse than that. I hurt him. I'm such an idiot."

"You're not an idiot," Mason says. "You're not over. If you were, he wouldn't have reacted like that. Go home. Get some sleep. We'll talk tomorrow."

I nod, hugging her gently before heading out. I walk back down the hallway. Everything sinking in.

Not just Kyle—all of it. Pushing Alex. An attempt to protect myself in the worst way. Letting my emotions spiral.

And now? I regret every damn second of it.

I saw his face tonight, not just anger, nor jealousy. Something deeper.

Hurt, maybe even betrayal.

I descend the stairs without acknowledging Riddick. Nor Alex.

The final nail's coming; I can feel it. I head back to my room, too distraught, too angry.

Roarke is waiting. Arms crossed, his expression unreadable. But I know that look. He's frustrated. Tired. Done.

"Andy, do you fucking want him or not?"

His voice is razor-sharp. His tone shocks me. I blink, thrown. Even when he's mad, Roarke is never like this.

Instinctively, I take a step back. "I don't want Kyle," I say. He gives me a knowing look.

"You and Alex are going to make it work, or you are going to be done. I can't keep dealing with this shit between you two."

"You act like I have a choice," I bite back. "Elitus is clear, you know that."

"Fuck Elitus. Do you think I like the rules any more than you do? Watching everyone, I give a damn about getting twisted up, because some bureaucratic assholes think they can control who we love?"

He shakes his head. "I don't have the answers, Andy. But I know this: Alex isn't walking away from you. Not really. So, tell him you are done and walk away from him for good... or tell him you're all in and the two of you fight like hell to make it work."

My throat tightens. "What if he won't fight for me?"

Roarke's gaze softens, but his voice stays firm. "Then he's not the guy you think he is."

I can't stop the tears. Roarke steps forward and pulls me into a strong, familiar hug. "I love him," I whisper.

"No shit," Roarke says.

I manage a watery smile.

But it fades fast.

Because no matter what I want...

I might've pushed him too far.

"Do you want me to kick his ass?" Roarke asks.

"I thought you two were best buds again?"

"He's my best friend," he tells me, "but you're my twin. I want you both to be happy, not miserable wrecks. If he comes to talk to you, listen. I know it's hard for you to keep that smart mouth in check but make an attempt."

I wipe my eyes. "I will try."

SIXTEEN

Alex

When Riddick brings me to the Millers', I spot Andy with Mason. I decided to wait. She doesn't need more stress tonight. And neither does Mason.

But before I can settle, my father steps through the door. His posture is rigid, eyes sharp.

I already know he will not let me off the hook. He jerks his head toward the porch. I follow.

The night's weight clings to me; body tense, mind still spinning.

The second we step outside; he starts in on me. "What the fuck happened, Alexander?"

I exhale hard, raking my hand through my hair. My head pounds, body still wired from the fight, from everything. I can't look at him yet, so I focus on the ground, trying to find the words.

"I was stupid. I don't know. Shit—Mason will be fine, but this was all my fault. I fucking saw Ross put his hands on her, and I lost it."

His entire stance shifts. "He put his hands on your sister?"

"No, shit, no ...Andy."

Silence. That's worse than yelling. He stares at me, unreadable, but it presses hard against my chest.

"Alex, you need to decide what you want. If you want the girl, you need to make a stand."

"What, just open the floodgates for everyone? Elitus has made their opinion crystal clear."

"And it's not helping," he snaps. "I know damn well they're all chasing Mason. And Charley. And every other girl. Damn it, Alex. Just be smart. If you want her, then tell her. Don't play games. It's not helping anyone. Especially if your sister ends up in the middle."

I freeze, studying him. "Are you saying what I think you're saying?"

His expression hardens. "Alex, how old are you?"

"Almost Twenty-Two."

"You've been a legal adult for years. Hell, in Virginia, I think you could've gotten married six years ago. Your mother and I were married by the time I was your age. Maria had two kids by then."

"But—"

"No, but," his voice cuts through me, firm. "I can't tell you how proud I am of the man you've become. But dammit, Alex, you've got to fight for yourself, for what you want. What they want. You're their leader—not just because you're the oldest, but because you're my son. They look to you for direction. Maybe not on the field—that's your sister's turf. But everywhere else. Even McGuire listens when you talk occasionally."

The words hit deep. I've always known Dad was proud of me, but this is different. This feels like permission.

Like he's giving me space to challenge everything I was bred for.

"How though?" My voice comes out rough. "I don't know how. Trust me, I've thought about it for so long I don't even remember when I didn't."

"Be honest. That's all I can tell you." His expression softens. "Mason would say the same—she hates secrets and bullshit. I can get you in front of Elitus. If you bring it forward, I will back you. Others will too. Hell, your mothers have been lecturing me about this for years."

"And then what? We just let it turn into a free-for-all. Not that it would, but still."

Robert sighs, frustration clear. "Alex, I can't answer that. But I know tonight can't happen again. And it will, maybe not with someone who has your ability, but with someone else's."

"We know what the labs say. Aggression, tension. It's all tied to your X and hormones. It makes you incredible weapons. But also, liabilities. Especially when you lose control."

I stay silent, not knowing how to respond.

"I'm going to check on your sister," he says. "You've got fences to mend. I haven't told your mother—she'll be furious. Maria will say, 'I told you so.'"

He squeezes my shoulder, his grip solid. It's the support I didn't know I needed. A reminder that despite all the rules Elitus has tried to force down our throats, my father still believes in choice. In my ability to change things.

I head back inside and find Riddick. He's waiting.

I know he won't leave until Mason's ready.

Andy comes downstairs not long after. She doesn't even look at me as she passes.

I should stop her. But I let her port out. I know I'll deal with her after I check on Mason.

Once my father has checked on Mason, I head up. I know she should be fine by now, but her armor's up. Those impenetrable shields she's been leaning on more lately.

"Mason, I'm so sorry."

"Don't be. It was an accident. You need to learn more control, Alex," she laughs.

I roll my eyes. "Oh, come on. You know that wasn't just an accident. That was me losing my shit."

Truth is, I wasn't even mad at Kyle. I was aggravated and jealous that I wasn't the one with her. She smirks. "Well, at least you're admitting it. Progress."

I sit beside her. She reaches out, squeezing my hand.

"You and I are a lot alike, Alex. We want to change things. We aspire to be more than they expect. You're my big brother. I respect the hell out of you. But you've got to fight for more than what they allow."

"I know," I admit. "I'm going to talk to Elitus and push for change."

"Good," she says, nodding. "And Andy?"

I exhale. "I need to figure out how to fix that, too."

Mason squeezes my hand tighter. "Be honest with her. Take care of her. She doesn't need you to play the hero, Alex. She just needs you to fight for her."

I nod, taking in her words. "Because it's fate?"

She smirks. "You know it."

For the first time all night, I breathe a little easier.

Andy

After a long shower, I step out of the bathroom. Steam clings to my skin; the heat does not ease the tension in my muscles.

All I want is to crawl into bed, bury myself under the blankets, and pretend the world doesn't exist.

But someone's already sitting on my bed waiting.

Alex.

He's hunched over, elbows on his knees, head in his hands.

He looks exhausted. Defeated. The sight cuts straight through me. I grip the doorframe, sighing. This conversation was always coming.

When he lifts his head, eyes meet mine—dark, heavy with emotion.

I shake my head. How did we end up like this?

"What do you want, Alex?" I whisper, already knowing the answer.

He's come to say goodbye. Tears slip down my cheeks before I can stop them.

He stands, and I don't even realize I'm moving back until my back hits the wall. But he doesn't stop. He keeps coming, his presence wrapping around me as his shields do.

I can't run. I don't want to.

Then, his mouth is on mine. The kiss is electric. A desperate need that feels as if I am being consumed by a fire I can't control.

His hands slide into my damp hair, pulling me closer, deepening the kiss, like he's afraid I'll disappear if he lets go.

My fingers fist in his shirt, tugging him closer, trying to fuse myself to him.

This is my man, the one I dream about. The one I ache for every night.

His hands are everywhere; under my shirt, gripping my hips, pressing into my lower back as he grinds against me.

His need is raw. Urgent.

A shudder rips through me. My body aches.

I lift and hook my leg around his waist; he lifts me like I weigh nothing, pinning me to the wall.

I rock against him, feeling the hard length against my core.

He groans into my mouth—deep, needy. The sound makes me tremble.

He's holding nothing back, unleashing every ounce of tension, longing, the unbearable need that has been between us for so long.

He kisses me like he's starving. Like he's dying without me.

And I feel it everywhere, my skin, soul, the ache between my thighs.

When I bite his lip, he groans. His hands tighten on my ass, dragging me harder against him.

Heat crashes through me. Blinding and overwhelming.

My mind spirals, lost in him. The way he fits, the way he makes everything else disappear.

I pant against his lips, shaking. Then I feel it. The crackle of energy between us, raw and uncontrolled.

His shields flicker, shifting under the weight of everything we've held back.

My power rises—not for combat, but with need.

It surges between us, feeding on emotion, on years of tension, on the unbearable weight of wanting what we could never have.

The world outside disappears. It's just us, a battle of restraint and surrender.

"Alex," I moan his name as I come apart, my head falling back against the wall, pleasure rippling through me in dizzying waves.

He holds me steady, breath ragged, forehead pressed to mine.

For a long moment, neither of us speaks.

We exist. Caught between past mistakes and an uncertain future; clinging to each other like lifelines.

He lowers me back to the floor, his arms still locked around me, like letting me go might break something.

I want to say something, but the words won't come.

I don't even know what this means. "Andy," he breathes, pressing a kiss to my temple.

I sigh, my hands smoothing over his shoulders to ground myself.

He steps back but doesn't release me. His gaze lingers on my face; it's full of longing, and some inner war I can't quite name.

But beneath it, there's something else. Relief.

"My father," he says, voice low but steady. "He's going to back me. I'm going to Elitus. I'm going to ask them to drop the ban."

"Oh." The word slips from my lips, my mind still struggling to catch up.

"I should stay away from you until I talk to them," he says, exhaling. "I should."

He smirks, but it's weak. "Roarke's next door, Mason's down, and honestly? I'm fucking exhausted. So, if you don't mind climbing a few stairs... I'd like it if you came up with me."

A laugh bubbles up before I can stop it. There's something in his eyes: hope, determination, and need. That makes my chest tighten. Suddenly, it feels like someone flipped a switch between us. How? Why? I don't care.

So much has been uncertain, but not this need. This connection.

"So, I'm just supposed to forgive you? Just like that?" I raise an eyebrow. Part of me wants to keep the wall up—to make him feel the sting of every moment he left me wondering. But looking at him now? Exhausted, open, and trying. I can't. Not when this feels like the first honest moment we have had in forever.

His face falls. "Oh shit, that was a joke. Alex, I don't know where we go from here... but I know I don't want to go backward."

Relief flickers through his eyes first, softening everything about him. Then the tension in his jaw, the line of his shoulders. The smirk that follows isn't sharp or guarded like before. It's real. Open.

"For now... we go to my bed." He says, my eyebrows shoot up.

"No—wait," he groans. "Damn it, now you've got me saying everything wrong." He laughs, breathless. "I just want to hold you. We can take everything else slow."

He glances at the door. "Roarke will kick my ass if we stay much longer. He's not blocking me, but he knows we both need more practice shielding." His gaze softens as he looks at me. "So, what do you say?"

I shake my head, amusement tugging at my lips. "I think I'm going too easy on you."

"You can be mad at me tomorrow about something else," he says with a grin, pulling me in for a quick kiss. Just a brush of lips at first. But the second we touch, it unravels. The tension we've both been carrying melts into something else, hungrier, rougher, like we're trying to replace every second we lost.

But then, as it turns more desperate, I feel it, the pinprick.

I pull back, glancing at his hands.

"Fuck." His energy is spiking, his shields unstable, and they are off from everything tonight.

"Are you going to be, okay?" I ask, concern slipping into my voice.

"Yeah," he says, though he looks worn. "I'm tired. Everything's a mess... but Riddick and Mason will help." He glances at me, voice softening. "Don't worry. Seems like everyone's been rooting for us."

I offer a small smile. But deep down, I know things between us are still far from settled.

The issue is more complex than just Elitus and the dating ban. It's about trusting that this version of him, the one who reached for me, who asks instead of deciding for me, that this version stays. That we make this work, and part of me knows. Maybe he's finally choosing me, not despite everything, but because of it.

Alex

"You want me to come with you?" Mason asks, sitting beside Andy on my bed. She stretches out like she doesn't have a care in the world—but I know better. Roarke stands by the door, arms crossed, watching it all unfold.

I'm more nervous than I should be.

I can handle this.

Who am I kidding? This is going to be a disaster.

And worse, I'm putting Andy at risk.

"It'll be fine," Andy reassures me, flashing that lopsided grin that always loosens something in my chest. "I believe in you."

Mason snickers beside her. "That makes one of us."

Roarke exhales. "Whatever happens, we'll handle it. I'll make sure none of it blows back on Andy."

Andy shifts, eyes narrowing, a spark of defiance lighting in her face. "What's that supposed to mean?"

Roarke doesn't flinch.

"Andy, what do you think happens when people find out you're in a relationship with Alex?"

The insinuation is clear, and I don't fucking like it.

My temper spikes, but before I can say anything, something shifts.

Fear. Not mine. Not Roarke's.

Andy's.

It's subtle, just a flicker of dread. Mason feels it too; she turns to Andy, watching her.

I glance at Roarke. He's not surprised by her reaction, which pisses me off even more.

I need to ask her about it. But later.

A knock at the door interrupts my thoughts before I can push further. I exhale, forcing my shoulders to relax, one thing at a time.

Roarke opens the door, and Riddick steps in, cocky smirk in place.

Mason scowls. She's mad about something as usual. Dad said she's healed and cleared for duty; it's at least one thing I don't have to worry about.

"What's up?" I ask, not in the mood for whatever bullshit Riddick's bringing.

"I'm your backup," he replies.

"Do I need it?"

"You're not facing the Elitus firing squad alone," he shrugs. "Besides—it'll piss McGuire off that not only Robert backs you. But Stephen as well."

Even Roarke lifts an eyebrow. "You went to your dad?" Andy asks, just as surprised.

"Well, I went to my mom first, and she made him see reason. Just like Maria and Joanne did. Fairly sure, the mommy squad gave them a heads-up."

I sigh. That could be good... or bad.

Part of me wanted to blindside them. But if they're already talking about it, maybe that's not the worst outcome.

I nod at Riddick, then turn to Andy and pull her into a quick kiss.

She's still tense, too tense. I hate leaving things like this.

"We'll talk when I get back, okay?" I murmur, brushing my thumb over her cheek.

She smiles, but there's hesitation in her eyes. Roarke meets my gaze and nods—his silent way of saying he's got her.

Mason follows us out into the hall, arms crossed. "I'd go with you, but that'd guarantee a 'no'."

Riddick grins. "Don't worry, I'm sure you'll reap the benefits if he pulls this off."

Mason's eyes narrow. "What the fuck is that supposed to mean?"

"Nothing," Riddick says, baiting her.

Goddamn it, why is everyone stirring up shit today?

"He means nothing," I cut in before she explodes, shooting Riddick a sharp look.

Mason smirks, side-hugs me, then flips Riddick off, walking backwards as he teleports us across campus.

The moment we land, I turn to Riddick. "Why do you start shit with her?"

He smirks, unfazed. "You asking if I was starting shit? Or if I was giving you a heads-up about my intentions?" I glance at him. "Like how you gave Roarke one?"

It's a low blow, and he knows it. "No, I was pushing her. You were too busy trying to gut Kyle to notice Bastian and Mason."

I frown. "I know they went out with Andy and Kyle."

"Exactly. Sounds like a double date to me."

Shit. I didn't even think about that. No way. They've always been just friends, sure they flirt. Besides, Mason's too focused on training... right?

But even as I try to rationalize it, my gut twists. Bastian is the only one she's been normal with. And I know how guys look at Mason. Even Bastian.

The same way they've started looking at Mya.

The same way they've always looked at Andy.

I can feel the shift coming.

If the dating ban lifts, the floodgates won't just open for me and Andy.

It'll be every guy with a pulse making a move.

And my sisters? They're prime targets. I hate that.

I glance at Riddick, catching the way his jaw tightens. He's trying to act indifferent, but I see through it. The way he talks about Mason, his irritation spikes even mentioning Bastian in the same sentence as her. He's not as detached as he pretends to be.

"She's not dating Bastian," I say, to see how he reacts.

His head snaps toward me. "I didn't say she was."

"You didn't have to."

He scoffs, shaking his head. "Mason does what she wants."

"That's the problem, isn't it?" I press. His silence is enough of an answer. For once, I'm grateful Mason's still focused on training.

What if the dating ban lifts?

The chaos that follows will make this look tame. That's what lingers as we move across campus. This isn't just about me and Andy.

It's about all of us.

If I'm walking into that room to ask them to rewrite the rules—to bend, to change, to allow for a future—then I need to be clear.

This is a plan. Not a plea. Lifting the ban changes everything.

Some of it will be good, but some of it?

Will be messy. Dangerous.

When you take power away from people who are used to controlling every part of your life, they don't just let go. They find new ways to take it back.

I'm about to make waves. I just hope I can survive the storm that follows.

My father brings me into the Elitus boardroom, Riddick beside me. We present our case; what we need, what I need. I don't shy away from their stares; I expect disappointment, but I don't see it. I see Elitus board members exchanging glances. Some of them already knew this was coming.

As suspected, McGuire and Thompson are not receptive. But with my father and Stephen behind us, they agreed to a closed session for review—parents included.

We step outside and wait. To stay calm, Riddick and I chat. He's trying to keep me distracted, to keep my mind from spinning, from overthinking. He knows I've got more riding on this than anyone.

I'm already thinking of contingency plans, running scenarios. What happens if they say no? I won't walk away. Not now.

So then what?

I fight. I keep fighting.

That's what.

SEVENTEEN

Alex

After a couple of hours, Elitus finishes the session and summons the four Gen Ones to lay everything out. But not what I expected.

Yes, they're giving up some control over our lives.

But of course, that's not all.

They also wanted to integrate Wights into the Elitus board and have each Gen One take a role in future projects and progression. Establish a way for structured input on everything from training to policy. It's a total shift in how things have always been done. They're letting us define our future.

That's why we're buried in work. For the last several hours; Kate, Wyatt, Kyle, and I have been working on our assignment.

Riddick left to update Andy and Roarke.

The upside? Kate's too busy organizing to argue with anyone.

I don't think she's eaten in hours, but I'm not about to stop her. If she wants to manage logistics, be my guest. She thrives on control, and I have no problem letting her tell me what to do.

They gave the responsibility to Gen Ones, but we're already working to bring others in.

Kate suggested forming committees on the key topics. In addition, Elitus opened six new board positions for Wights with no graduation requirement. That means some Gen Twos, Threes, and even Fours could have a say.

Gen Four won't care, but I know a few Gen Twos and Threes that would like a chance. At least the level-headed ones.

Kate glances up from her notes, her pen tapping against the table. "So, there will need to be four primary groups—general housing and residential, social and community events, academics, and training."

Wyatt, Kyle, and I are just here for decoration at this point. "Yes?" she presses.

We all nod. "Great. I'll oversee everything, but I need each of you to lead a section. Alex, I'll be nice and take the social events one. Wyatt gets academics, Kyle takes training—which leaves you with residential."

Thank God for that.

"We can call a meeting tomorrow," she continues.

"Tonight," I say. I have been away from Andy for too long, and I'm done waiting. It's time to move forward.

"Tonight?" She checks her watch, realizing how long we have been at it. Yes, Kate, we've been here for five hours. You've lost it.

Kyle checked out a while ago. He summoned a chessboard for Wyatt and himself.

"Tonight," I repeat. "I'm not waiting. We can at least introduce the idea and give everyone advance notice. Then you can figure out how people will apply to or join committees. It also gives them time to think about it. I know it adds more to Gen Two's plate with graduation coming, but at least it gives them options."

"I don't care either way," Kyle says, stretching. "I just want to ensure we get a say in who joins these committees. I'm not letting some idiot redesign training if they're not combat-enabled."

"I've got some ideas," I tell him. "I'll work it out with Calvin and a few others."

"Okay, well—since you want it tonight, you can coordinate that," Kate says, already standing. "I need to change. I guess we'll hold it in the auditorium?"

Aggravated but focused, I texted Bastian asking him to send out a campus-wide mental command.

Kate volunteers Kyle and me to inform Elitus.

Kyle abandons his chess game. Following me to find our fathers, both knee-deep in lab work.

In the last couple of hours, Kyle and I came to a mutual understanding. Neither of us holds a grudge for the prior night's events. We both take equal blame for Mason getting hurt. I know he wasn't serious about Andy, and we both agree that it's in the past. I should be more pissed, but I suspect Kyle knew I needed the push to make changes. I may never have gone to Elitus otherwise. And since it seems to have worked, I can't complain about the results.

Lab 2 is busy when we enter. The hum of machines, low voices, and the sharp scent of sterile metal and ozone all feed into the controlled chaos of Elitus' latest project. I spot them; Kyle's dad, mine, Dr. Miller, and Pepe, the heavy hitters.

Kyle and I weave through the clusters of researchers and technicians, sidestepping a group analyzing data screens filled with neural mapping displays.

The air crackles with urgency, the kind that comes with a breakthrough.

They've been making real advancements.

Pepe spots us first, offering a small smile as we approach. I hand over the packet—plans for everything, or at least a working outline, condensed into something actionable.

Pepe flips through the pages, nodding. "That was fast work."

"I'd love to take credit, but it's all Kate. We follow her instructions."

Kyle snorts. "Understatement of the year."

Pepe chuckles, shaking his head.

Dr. Miller—Reese's dad—chimes in next, "Looks like a successful start. I'm sure you'll iron it out."

Robert skims the summary, already sliding into decision-making mode.

"I'll review it with the rest of Elitus tomorrow. If you and Kate can complete the committee members and expectations by next week's full meeting, that would be ideal."

Then he pauses, glancing up at me with that knowing look. "I don't want to assume—but are you going to bring up lifting the dating ban?"

Kyle side-eyes me. I can practically hear the silent commentary spinning in his head. I may have forgotten to mention that part of the changes to Gen Ones.

Elitus didn't mention it when they handed us this project. But it's been hanging over us for too long. It needs to be addressed. I nod.

"Yeah. I'll present it. Let them know that while it's being lifted, there will be rules—and we'll go over those. I'll also outline plans for off-campus events and integration. Make sure they understand the expectations. It's a step toward what many people have been waiting for."

Kyle leans in, arms crossed. "Are you reopening combat applications?"

We both know some people got denied in the first round and want back in.

"That's McGuire's call. He's still managing all contracts, mission teams, and enabling of combatants."

Of course he is. Control is his comfort zone. At least we're getting something out of this.

Pepe nods. "We'll draft an email to the parents and faculty. Get ahead of the fallout."

With that, we're dismissed.

Kyle and I head across the quad. The cool evening air is a welcome relief after the lab's heat. Campus lights stretch long shadows across the worn paths.

Kyle waits until we're out of earshot before he smirks. "So... is dating open just to you? Or everyone?"

I stop walking. "Kyle." Damn it, I should've seen this coming. I know he's not hinting at Andy. But my sister.

Kyle's always been a flirt, but he and Mason? They've always been close—battle partners, Tier Three trainers. Tier Three bonds pull the strongest to each other. For Kyle and Mason, both hitting X regularly, it's hard to avoid.

He was her main mentor when she was younger, but after she joined combat, he backed off.

Still, I know he is interested. They all are.

He lifts his hands, all innocence. "Hey, I have to worry too," he shrugs at my glare. "Charley's worse than Mason half the time. And I'm sure Paige is going to chase David."

I shake my head. "No—it's open to everyone. But we need to make the rules crystal clear. This could go sideways fast. Too many people in the dorms already, and that's not counting outsiders who think they have a shot with the girls."

Kyle snorts. "Yeah, that won't end in disaster at all."

I roll my shoulders, trying to shake off the tension. "Mason turns twenty in a couple of months. She's already a legal adult. The rest of Gen Three isn't far behind."

And that doesn't even count my other two sisters, both seventeen.

Aimee is still at home, but she's eager, just waiting to break out of our mom's house.

Mya's been relentless, throwing herself into training, pushing harder than anyone. She's essentially a clone of Mason; driven, methodical, and deadly.

And it's working. If Mya keeps this up, she'll be on mission dockets soon enough, especially given how close she is to clearing High Two and X Three levels.

Kyle studies me for a beat. "You think the ban lifting is going to be a problem?"

I let out a dry laugh. "I don't know; there is as much risk as reward—for some of them, at least."

Kyle contemplates as he kicks a rock loose, watching it skitter down the path. "I think we just need to proceed with caution—but this is a good thing. Aimee and the others will be psyched if you get new resident buildings approved." He adds, changing the subject, "They're dying to move out of their parents' houses."

I groan. "Don't remind me. If we don't get the right people on that committee, we'll end up with frat houses and luxury condos."

Kyle smirks. "You say that like it's a bad thing."

"It is a bad thing. We need structure."

"Not everyone thrives under structure, Alex." He gives me a pointed look. "Some of us do better when we're not suffocating."

That's the difference between us. I lead through control. Through organization. By making sure every damn piece fits the bigger picture.

Kyle leads with instinct. With trust. He makes people feel like they belong—like they can handle whatever comes their way.

That's why people look to him in the field. He's the one you want at your side when shit goes sideways.

Kyle snickers, "You won't admit it, but even if this is rocky at first... these changes? They're the right move. That's why people look up to you. Even I do... sometimes."

I blink, surprised. Kyle never says shit like this.

I shake my head. "I may lead here, but in the field, they still look to you."

Kyle scoffs. "Yeah, right. We both know who leads out there. She may defer to me on missions but trust me—she leads us."

I glance at him.

He's lost in thought. He's thinking about Mason.

Just like Riddick.

Just like Bastian.

And every other goddamn guy circling her, waiting for an opening.

It grates on me more than it should.

Mason doesn't see it. Or maybe she does—and just doesn't care. But there's a reason guys look at her like she's a goddamn prize.

Eventually, one of them is going to make a move. That thought knots in my gut, a mix of protectiveness and frustration.

Mason can handle herself; I know that. But this kind of attention? It turns into a distraction, a complication. And I don't trust half of these guys to have her best interests in mind.

Kyle must catch my expression, because he smirks. "You can't guard her forever, you know."

I exhale, rubbing my temples. "I don't want to guard her. I don't want to deal with the fallout when shit inevitably blows up."

He laughs. "Right. Because Mason's never been the center of drama before."

I scowl. But he's not wrong.

Still enough about Mason. That's not my focus right now.

Andy is. For the first time in way too long, I don't have to hide what I want. No second-guessing. With no rules in the way. I can be with her.

And after everything: months of pushing, waiting, wanting, I need to see her. Now.

"I'm done with this conversation," I mutter, already changing course, heading toward the dorms with a new purpose.

Kyle chuckles, falling into step beside me. "Ah. Now I see. You've got places to be. Or rather, someone to be with."

When I enter the dorms, the energy slams into me—buzzing with excitement, rumors already swirling. What catches my eye?

Cases of beer and liquor bottles lined up on the counter like trophies.

"Alex!" Aimee shouts from across the room, stacking red cups as she organizes the bar. "Mason said we can have a party!"

Mya smirks from her spot against the back of the couch, enjoying my reaction. I exhale, already bracing for whatever excuse Mason's about to serve up. I scan the room and spot her near the kitchen, in deep discussion with Charley. Tilting my head, I signal for her to join me.

She catches the cue, but she doesn't come alone. Charley trails behind her. Kyle joins as well; he never misses a chance to stir the pot.

I cross my arms the second she stops in front of me. "Are you trying to get our privileges revoked in one night?"

Her frown is instantaneous. Shit, I know that look. Before she can fire back, I sigh and shake my head. "I'm sorry—that came out wrong. I didn't mean to blame you."

Her shoulders drop a notch, but she's still studying me.

"Honestly," I say, softer this time, "I'm glad you're being social. I thought 'Robot Mason' was here to stay." I use Mya's nickname for her, hoping to defuse the tension.

Mason rolls her eyes but doesn't bite. "Don't worry. I already set down the ground rules. Jasper and Siobhan are on shields, and aside from people with siblings in the dorms, this isn't an open house. We'll plan a proper event later this week, but come on, Alex—when's the last time we celebrated? This is like Independence Day," she says, grinning.

Kyle studies her, arms crossed, his expression unreadable. If anyone sees through Mason's bullshit faster than I do, it's him.

"Are you drinking?" Kyle asks.

"Yes, but not to excess." She arches a brow. "Why? Are you looking for a rematch?"

Kyle smirks, but before he can answer, Riddick strolls in, passing by Charley, and heads straight for the fridge. Riddick barely acknowledges anyone as he grabs a snack, tearing it open; only for Charley to snatch the cheese stick from his hand and shove it in her mouth.

Riddick glares at her. Mason grins and smacks his arm.

"Was that a dare?" Kyle asks, amusement flickering in his eyes.

Mason laughs, shaking her head as she grabs another snack. She hands it to Riddick this time. No, Charley interference.

Riddick unwraps it but doesn't eat. Instead, he angles toward Kyle. "You really want to go down that road again?"

They never back down when there is a challenge. And while Kyle likes to think he's hot shit, he can't hold his liquor, not like Riddick, and definitely not like Mason.

Kyle smirks. "I mean, if you're offering."

Mason groans. "No. Absolutely not. I am not playing referee again."

Riddick glances at her. "You weren't a referee, Mason. You saved his ass."

Kyle scoffs. "Saved me? I had that in the bag."

Mason turns to face him. "Kyle, you blacked out after fifty-two shots."

He lifts a shoulder in a lazy shrug. "Could've kept going."

Riddick takes a bite of his snack, shaking his head. "Bullshit."

Kyle narrows his eyes. "Says the guy who stopped right after me."

Mason sighs. "Yeah, and the difference? Riddick wasn't scheduled to fight in the arena the next morning."

Kyle goes silent for a beat, his smirk faltering. "Wait—that's why you stopped it?"

Mason shrugs. Kyle exhales and rubs the back of his neck. "I would've been fine."

Riddick smirks, though there's an edge to it. "Sure. You couldn't stand, but yeah—totally fine."

Mason glares at them both. "If you two want to dick-measure, do it in the training room—not over a hundred-proof contest of stupidity."

Kyle crosses his arms, smug. "What, worried I'll win this time?"

Mason exhales. "I swear, if you two start this again, I will lock you in a shielded room and force you to watch Siobhan's K-Drama marathons."

Kyle grimaces. "That's low, Mason."

Riddick shakes his head. "Brutal."

Mason shrugs. "Try me."

Kyle and Riddick exchange a look. For a second, I think one of them might actually push it—just for the hell of it.

Charley, who's been quietly observing, grins. "I think they should. It's been a while since we had real entertainment."

Mason tosses her empty water bottle into the trash, eyes both, then smirks. "Fine. But no bullshit rules this time. If we do this, we do it right."

Riddick's gaze sharpens. "You're considering it?"

Mason winks. "Why? You scared?"

Kyle lets out a laugh. "Now that's a dare."

Before Mason can respond, I've already decided—I've had enough. I turn to leave, heading toward Andy's room, until Mason catches my arm.

"Alex," she breathes, her voice edged with concern. She falls into step beside me, her voice dropping, the chaos of the pre-party fading behind us. "Use what I showed you. It won't hold perfectly, and Roarke and I aren't shielding you through sex, so just... pace yourselves."

She hesitates, then sighs. "Take it slow, okay? I know she's chomping at the bit to move forward, but you two just got back together. Don't let this turn into a sprint."

I nod, appreciating the honesty. "You're a good friend."

She smirks, her walls snapping back into place. "And you're a great big brother—but I'll deny it if you ever say that out loud."

I chuckle; she pulls me into a quick hug.

"Alex," she murmurs, her voice quieter now. "You did well today. Tonight. I know it wasn't easy, but we need it."

Exhaling while I run a hand through my hair. "I don't think the next couple of weeks will be easy, either."

"Probably not," she agrees. "But we'll adjust."

She steps back and nods toward the room.

"Go see Andy," she says. "She's waiting for you."

That's all the motivation I need.

EIGHTEEN

Andy

Hand in hand, Alex and I step into the auditorium. For a moment, the entire room falls silent. Then hushed murmurs spread among the crowd.

I can't help but smile. Normally, I hate being the center of attention, especially in a room this full, but right now, it's necessary.

We are making a statement; that Alex, of all people, is okay with being this open? It's surreal.

Just a few days ago, he wouldn't even have been in the same room as me. Not that I made it easy for him; I avoided him just as much. But this is different—real.

He leads me toward the front row, where Mason has saved me a seat between her and Roarke. Nerves twist in my stomach. Alex looks at ease, shoulders relaxed, jaw set with muted confidence, like none of this fazes him. I do not know how he does it.

Before I can sit, he tugs me back against him. My breath catches.

Then he kisses me.

Not a quick, subtle kiss. But one meant to prove a point.

This kiss is all heat, intensity. Raw and consuming, like he's been waiting too long and refuses to hold back any longer.

Alex isn't one for grand gestures. If I didn't feel the heat simmering beneath my palms that rest on his chest, then I'd think he was putting on a show. But he's not.

I melt into it, oblivious to the world, until a sharp mental nudge slams into my shield, snapping me back to reality.

Roarke.

Oh, God.

We're making out in front of a hundred people.

Oops.

The crowd erupts in cheers and whistles. My face flames. Mason groans and kicks her brother in the shin as I pull away, mortified, and sink into my seat. The entire front row, our closest friends, are laughing, all too entertained by the spectacle.

Roarke shakes his head at me, but there's a small smile tugging at his lips. A hint of a smile that hasn't appeared in weeks. I'm not sure what has been weighing on him, but now that my drama is dying, maybe he can find his way back to himself.

Mason looks relaxed. For once, she's not vibrating with stress or ready to snap. And damn, I missed my friend.

Alex steps onto the stage, seizing the room's focus. His voice cuts through the lingering chatter—steady, composed.

"We've asked you all here for some excellent news."

The murmurs fall away, tension replacing idle curiosity.

"Elitus, after much deliberation—and some pressure from myself and others—has finally agreed it's time to plan for a future beyond just missions and science." His gaze sweeps over the crowd. "Starting this week, we'll be forming committees in a variety of focus areas. Kate will walk through the process shortly. Also, Elitus is opening applications for six Wight members to join the Elitus board."

The room stirs, low voices, surprised glances. Elitus never gives up this much control. Kyle stands next to Alex. "Details on the selection process will be released soon. It's open to all Gen Ones, Twos, and Threes." He pauses. "Kate will break down the committee groups and high-level goals. We wanted everyone here in case there were questions."

Then, more seriously, "We specifically asked Elitus not to attend. This is about building a more cohesive unit, our unit."

We all know what that means. For the first time, we will have a say in what comes next. It's terrifying; no pre-written path, no one telling us where to go or how to get there.

I glance at Alex, calm, in control, every inch the leader. The weight of this is on him now. I believe in him and know he's capable. I also know he pushes himself harder than anyone should.

Kate steps forward, PowerPoint already queued up. She's polished and efficient, her presence commanding in a way that makes even the most restless people settle down and listen.

It's one of the many things I admire; she can walk into any room and command it.

This changes everything, not just for Alex, but for all of us. For my sisters. For my friends.

Delilah is still stuck at home, and even though she won't say it outright, I know she hates it there. I asked Roarke if we could move her into the dorms, but he doesn't want to leave Ava behind, not alone. Maybe this new residential committee can help with that.

But what about my parents? My mom was at the meeting earlier. It feels like a lifetime ago, and I haven't heard from her since.

Will she call? Will she tell my dad? I don't know how he'll react. I don't want to know.

We barely speak. I avoid going home whenever I can. And he's all but disowned me. He won't care about the changes to Elitus; he's not part of that world anymore. What he will care about is Alex and me; what people will say.

I swallow hard as my pulse kicks up. If he hears about this secondhand, it'll only make things worse. But what the hell am I supposed to say?

Hey, Dad—remember how you've dictated what I should do and who I should be with? Yeah, well, Alex and I are together. And I don't need your permission.

That would go over well. My hands tighten into fists in my lap, and I force my focus back to the presentation.

Kate is still listing committee options. Around me, a few people murmur, already tossing around ideas. The entire room feels different now, buzzing, alive.

Alex steps forward again, finding me before he starts. "In case you missed the memo earlier," amusement in his voice, "Elitus has agreed to remove the ban on dating and social interactions."

The room erupts. I can hardly hear him over the noise.

"But," he continues, "not without limits. This includes off-campus events and more freedom in coming and going—but all of it—comes with guidelines we'll help define."

I exhale slowly, trying to keep my expression neutral. I should be thrilled. Part of me is, but another part that is trained to expect things to go wrong can't shake the nerves creeping up my spine like static.

Especially when my father finds out.

Kurt Parrish does not like surprises. What does he hate even more? Being disobeyed. He likes control, and when you deviate from the version he expects from you, it goes badly. That's why Roarke and I left home for the dorms the moment we could. Roarke saw what it was doing to me. He knew.

"Roarke's the only child I have worth a damn." That's what my father had told me, more than once.

He isn't just verbally abusive; he is volatile. He lost his temper on more than one occasion, and I know my mom took the brunt of his abuse. Kurt joined the Elitus guard, trying to prove he was more than just donor sperm. But his temper and lack of control held him back. Now, he's merely a footnote in the Elitus world. He blames everyone but himself. And his primary target for his own failures, Robert Clarke.

Roarke has always been close to Alex, but we never had him over. Not once. Kurt made his opinion of the Clarkes clear, Aimee included, even though she's De's best friend. So, yeah, Alex and me? We will be a problem.

I may be almost twenty-one. Graduation is weeks away. But sometimes it feels like the noose is already around my neck. One wrong step and it tightens.

I hate that feeling. But I also know I have to shield it. Push it down. Because if I don't, it'll take over. And for once, I want to be here. Be happy. Be whole.

I am still nervous about what all these changes mean for the Wights. But for the first time, the excitement outweighs the fear.

The energy in the air shifts, crackling, heavy, like something bigger than all of us is finally moving into place.

Alex wraps things up, but most of us linger. I watch the crowd break into small clusters of conversation while I wait for Alex to come down.

Across the room, Aimee, Mya, and Delilah are already making plans, disappearing toward the back doors like they're on a mission.

Roarke lets out a groan, jaw tightening as his eyes track them.

"Fucking Mya." His voice is low, clipped.

I smirk, nudging him with my elbow. "What? Delilah won't be a little girl forever, Roarke."

"I know, but Mya doesn't need to drag my sister into her shenanigans."

His frustration cuts deeper than usual—more than just big brother protectiveness. I arch a brow. "Shenanigans?" I ask with a teasing grin.

"Look, Delilah doesn't belong at one of these parties. I let her stay home for a reason." He exhales again. "And if Mya gets it in her head to 'corrupt' her, I swear to God, we're going to have a severe problem."

I let out a short laugh. "Roarke, Delilah is seventeen, not seven. You know she looks up to Mya, right? Hell, most of the younger girls do. It's not like Mya's going to throw her into the deep end."

Roarke scoffs, his whole body still tense. "You don't know Mya like I do."

There's something in his tone, not just annoyance. Something sharper, sadder. But he shuts it down before I can press.

That catches me off guard. "I think I know her pretty well."

His jaw flexes, but he says nothing. That isn't like him.

Before I can push further, he sighs. "Speaking of corruption, do me a favor?"

I cross my arms. "Depends."

"If you two are going to... you know...do things..."

I glare at him. "Oh my God, Roarke."

"Just sleep in his room," he finishes, unfazed. "It's already a pain in the ass blocking out all the rest of the dorms. At least until you learn to shield better, or Alex can cover you completely. You're a lost cause at keeping me out."

I groan, covering my face with my hands. "I cannot believe we are having this conversation right now."

"You're the one who asked about shenanigans."

"You are impossible. And I don't even know if Alex wants me there...."

Alex's voice rumbles from behind me. "Want you where?"

I turn just as he drops into the chair beside me. His presence grounds me. Mason is already wandering off to talk with Max and the others.

"In your bed," Roarke replies flatly before I can come up with a good lie. "It's too much next door."

I groan again. Alex just chuckles like Roarke isn't making my life hell.

"You know what I mean," Roarke mutters. "Anyway, I've got to go find my sister before she gets any ideas from Mya."

"Sorry we ruined your plans to go offsite to get a date," Marty teases as she arrives with her twin and David in tow to congratulate us.

"I don't date them," Roarke says dryly, nodding toward Charley and Mason. "You'll see. Can't wait to run into them at a bar."

Beside me, Alex is tense. His grip on my arm tightens—just slightly. But I feel a shift in his energy. His posture goes rigid.

"We're a little far from that," Alex says, standing and pulling me up with him. "Let's get through tonight first."

Alex

The second we step through the dorm doors, we're hit with it: bass-heavy music vibrating through the walls, a pulsing rhythm that sinks into my bones. It's loud, chaotic, and unrestrained.

The whole place is full. People are laughing, shouting, dancing, and stumbling through doorways. There's a poker game near the stairs, a drinking contest at the kitchen table, and an infectious energy I haven't felt in a long time.

The back doors are wide open, letting in crisp fall air that cuts through the heat of too many bodies crammed into one space.

Roarke steps in behind us, muttering under his breath. "Fucking hell."

His eyes scanned the room, zeroing in on Delilah like a guided missile. I don't even need to follow his line of sight. I know exactly where she is.

She's laughing with Mya and Aimee, enjoying her freedom. His jaw tightens, but he veers toward the bar without saying another word.

Wyatt stands like a sentinel by the bar, Kate perched on the stool beside him, arms crossed, a half-smile tugging at her mouth. Amused, observant. Classic Kate.

Kyle breezes past us on the way to the back door, smirking like this mayhem is the highlight of his entire month.

"Frat house?" He jokes.

"Feels like it," I mutter, shaking my head. But there's something else in my voice. It is lighter, easier. I feel like I can breathe.

I glance over. Andy is next to me. Her eyes are already on me; wide, curious, a little overwhelmed... and glowing. There's heat in her gaze, the one that knocks the air out of my lungs. And now she's mine.

Finally.

It doesn't feel real yet—not completely. But we're here. Together. No hiding. No bullshit.

Every time I look at her, it hits me all over again. This is what I should've been fighting for a year ago. Her. Us. A future that doesn't come with secrets or shame. I know I can't hold on to that regret, but I also know I need to make it up to her.

Across the room, Mason climbs onto the bar like she owns the place, commanding attention with a sharp, two-fingered whistle. The music stops, and everyone looks at her.

"Alright, assholes, listen up!" she calls, lifting her drink high. "Tonight, we celebrate!"

Riddick slides in beside us, handing shots to both me and Andy. Jared follows close behind, smirking, his usual energy humming beneath the surface.

"He may be modest," Mason continues, raising her glass, "but we have Alex to thank for finally growing a pair and standing up for all of us."

The crowd erupts in whistles and cheers. I roll my eyes, but I let her go on.

"And with that," she adds, louder now, "congratulations to Alex and Andy—the first official in-house couple."

A round of applause breaks out—whistles, laughter. Andy's cheeks flush, and a grin tugs at my mouth before I can stop.

Mason winks at the crowd. "Remember what I said. Behave. Control yourselves. And keep it in check." She raises her drink again. "Gen Four—if you mess this up, it's your last time here. So, with that being said... To our future!"

Glasses clink. A chorus of cheers rises. We knock the shots back. The burn is smooth, expensive stuff. Bastian's doing.

Warmth spreads through my chest, but not from the alcohol.

Andy leans into me, and I slide my arm around her shoulders, pulling her close. She fits, like she always has.

Riddick's saying something, but I don't catch it. I'm too focused on her. On this. On the weight that is being lifted.

Weeks of silence. Months of longing. Years of frustration. All the near-misses—every one of them led to this.

But I know it's not over. Not really.

This relationship is still fragile. Technically, we're allowed. I pushed for it and used my law degree and liaison status to make changes.

I made them admit their rules were outdated. Restrictive. Unfair.

It worked, and the ban is lifted. Most of the parents backed me, as did a decent amount of Elitus. It's progress.

McGuire? He's still watching, waiting for someone to slip so he can yank the rug out from under us.

Therefore, I still must protect this. The battle isn't over.

And that's fine. I'll fight for this a thousand times over.

Mason reappears with drinks, dragging us toward the couch in the corner. The party swirls around us, loud and wild, but in this space, it feels distant. Like we're watching from behind glass.

I scan the room, not out of paranoia—well, maybe a little—but mostly habit.

Roarke is behind the bar now, face tight, eyes fixed on Delilah. She's with Mya and Aimee, laughing like they don't know they are in trouble. They do, but they're just choosing to ignore it.

My gaze shifts to the Gen Threes at the table: Matt, Connor, and Adrian. Not my favorites, to say the least.

At least the Monroe Three are present. They'll keep things in check. Christian too. Even Wyatt and Riddick's younger brothers are sitting at the table.

It's strange seeing them all here. I forget how many Gen Threes and Fours missed out on this—left out of the fun because they weren't combat.

But not all of them belong here. There's a tension I don't like, too many smug expressions, too many glances aimed at combat recruits.

Something's brewing. Resentment? Jealousy, maybe?

I'll deal with it later.

Andy shifts beside me, tilting her head up to meet my gaze. "Can we escape?" she murmurs.

I don't hesitate. I smile, slow and easy, and tug her up with me.

Escape? Yeah.

That sounds perfect.

NINETEEN

Alex

The moment Andy asks if we can escape, I don't hesitate.

I take her hand without a word, our fingers weaving together like they've always known how to find each other in the dark. Her grip is firm, but there's a tremble in it. With a silent question, I answer with the steady certainty of my touch. She fits beside me like she's always meant to.

We slip out together through the crush of bodies, past laughter that's too loud and lights too bright. The air outside the crowded room is cooler. We breathe a little easier.

Each step up the stairs softens the world behind us. The thrum of bass fades into the distant beat. My boots echo with each plank; hers barely make a sound, just a whisper. The silence isn't empty. It's electric. Charged with something that simmered too long.

We reach my room; the tension feels tangible—like it's taken shape and is walking beside us.

The hallway is dim. Quieter. I feel her beside me, every breath, every tremor of her fingers. The latch turning is too loud in the silent room. The soft click as it closes behind us feels final, like something shifted. Then it's just us.

The room is dim; lit only by the soft amber glow of the desk lamp I left on earlier. The space is simple. Clean. Bed. Desk. Shelves stacked with files and books. A few untouched decorations my mother insisted I bring from home, a photo of Kennedy, my Elitus Medal, and old boxing gloves hanging from the back of my chair.

It's nothing special. But with Andy here... it matters.

There's something open in her gaze. Not fear. Softer. Fragile. A rare, unguarded part of her that makes my breath catch.

I move toward her with purpose; I reach for her hand again, curling my fingers around her wrist. She's warm and tense, and her pulse thrums.

"Hey," I murmur, brushing my thumb across the back of her hand. "Are you okay?"

She nods, but it's hesitant, the kind that doesn't quite believe itself.

Her lips part like she has something to say, but she doesn't. She glances down at our hands, then back at me. I don't rush her.

I lift my hand to her jaw, my touch featherlight. She leans in, instinctive. That small, sweet gesture says more than words ever could.

"Andy," I whisper.

Her gaze sharpens, locking with mine. In that moment, something clicks; like everything we've been dancing around, all the walls we had built, suddenly don't matter.

"I want this," she says quietly. "I just..." Her fingers tighten around mine. It's impossible not to see how vulnerable she is. "I don't know if I'll be..."

"If you'll be what?"

She shifts her weight, gnawing her bottom lip, tension coming off her in waves.

"I don't know if I'll be what you like," she says, so soft I almost miss it.

My stomach drops.

"Andy—"

She cuts me off before I can finish. "I don't have experience, Alex. I mean—we've had moments, but not like this. Not really. I don't want you to go slow just because you think I need you to. Or because you feel you should. I just—"

I step in and cup her face with both hands, not letting her finish her statement. I kiss her the way I have wanted to for months. Years.

Everything I've been holding back; I pour into it.

She melts into me, stealing my breath from my lungs. Her hands grip the front of my shirt, her tongue tangles with mine, uncertain at first, then confident, matching mine.

She twists her fingers in my shirt like she's afraid I'll disappear.

I won't.

Not this time.

This isn't about experience. Or perfect moments. Or expectations.

This is her.

The girl who challenges me at every turn. She pushed every button, every boundary, causing me to question everything I thought I knew about loyalty, rules, and control.

She pulls back a smidge, her breath uneven, eyes wide.

"I don't want you to feel like you have to fix me," she whispers.

I shake my head. "I don't."

She studies my face—still wary, like she's waiting for the catch.

"I don't want perfect, Andy," I say, voice rough. "I want you. All of you. However, that looks."

She exhales, a tiny laugh slipping out. Then she leans in. This time it's her kiss. Slower. Deeper. She's finally letting herself believe in us.

I guide her toward the bed with one hand on her back. Not rushing, just steady. We move together like we've done this before, like our bodies already know how to close the distance between us.

Because maybe they do.

Maybe this was always inevitable.

She stops short before we sit down. Her hands fly up to grip my arms, nails dig into my skin, and she reaches up on her toes to kiss me. Not tame. Not careful. A kiss full of promise and longing. All nerves forgotten.

She's breathless when I pull back just enough to rest my forehead against hers. "I want to go slow," I murmur, tracing my fingers along her cheek, down the column of her throat. "Not because I think you need me to. Not because I think you can't handle this. But because I want to. Because I want you."

Andy's breath hitches, her fingers tightening on my shirt.

"I've wanted no one like this," I continue, voice low, steady. "You don't have to prove anything to me, Andy. You never have."

Her eyes glisten, something raw flickering in them, and she exhales.

Before I say anything else, she moves.

She presses up onto her toes, arms looping around my neck as she kisses me again, harder this time, her body molding against mine like she's trying to erase the space between us.

I groan into her mouth, hands sliding down to her waist, gripping her tighter as I lie her down on the bed. She's not letting me take my time, not giving me a second to second-guess anything.

And, fuck, I love that about her.

When her head hits the pillow, she breaks the kiss just long enough to look up at me, lips swollen, chest rising and falling with each breath.

I brush a strand of hair behind her ear, my thumb tracing the curve of her cheek. "You sure?"

She nods. "Yes."

Still, I hesitate. "Andy—"

"I don't want to wait anymore," she whispers, her voice steadier now, surer. "Not after everything we've been through. Not when I finally have you."

Her words hit me harder than I expected.

Because she's right.

This moment—it's ours.

I kiss her again, hovering over her on the bed. I know with every part of me that this is just the beginning.

Andy

The moment Alex lowers me to the bed; our world narrows down to just him and me. Music, the echo of laughter, and the dull throb of life outside the room, fades. What matters now is the warmth of his hands on my skin, the way his body presses against mine, anchoring me in this moment. In him.

He surrounds me—his scent, that mix of clean soap and something uniquely him, curling through my senses. The solid heat of his chest brushes against mine, his warm breath ghosting across my lips just before he captures them again.

The kiss is slow, deliberate, and devastating in its tenderness. It's not just want. It's worship. He's tasting something sacred.

His hands trail down my sides with a reverence that makes me tremble. Every inch of skin he touches feels marked. Memorized. He moves with care but not caution—like he knows exactly what I need and will give me all of it, piece by piece.

I should be nervous. I am.

But not because of him. Because of me.

What if I don't know what to do?

What if I'm not what he wants?

What if I can't make him feel even a fraction of what he's making me feel right now?

Alex breaks the kiss, his body poised above mine, breathing hard. The weight of his gaze sends a shiver down my spine.

"You're overthinking," he murmurs, voice rough but gentle.

I let out a shaky breath, gripping his arms, and grounding myself in the warmth of his body. "I just... I don't want to disappoint you."

Something sharp flashes in his eyes, protective and dark. He shakes his head, his voice dropping into something deeper.

"Andy." My name on his lips feels like a promise. "You couldn't."

I part my lips to argue, but then his mouth is at my throat, tracing a slow, searing path down my skin. And words no longer matter.

His lips find my collarbone, a gasp slipping from my lips as he presses open-mouthed kisses along my neck, his tongue flicking against my pulse point before he nibbles at my skin.

I arch into him, fingers sliding into his hair, gripping him tighter. His body is solid against mine, muscles flexing as he shifts between my legs.

The pressure sends another shockwave through me, and I fight to keep my shields steady, to keep my emotions inside instead of broadcasting them like a goddamn beacon.

Because if I let go, let him feel everything I'm feeling right now, the entire dorm will know. Maybe part of me wants them to feel, to know I'm his.

Alex exhales sharply, his lips ghost over my jaw before he pulls back just enough to meet my eyes.

"You need to shield better," he warns, his lips brushing my jaw in a wicked tease.

I glare at him, breathless. "I'd like to see you try shielding when you're kissing me like that."

His smirk deepens and darkens, sending a fresh wave of heat pooling low in my stomach.

"Oh, I am," he murmurs, "but if you don't tighten yours, Roarke will pound on that door in about five seconds."

I groan, burying my face against his shoulder, trying to focus, trying to breathe.

But it's impossible.

Because then he's tugging my shirt up, his fingers grazing bare skin as he lifts it over my head. He tosses it aside without looking, and I'm already reaching behind to unhook my bra, adding it to the growing pile next to the bed.

His hands are on me immediately, exploring, mapping every inch of exposed skin.

When he leans down and draws one aching peak into his mouth, I cry out, my back arching off the bed, chasing the heat of him. His tongue swirls, lips firm and deliberate, and I can't think. Only feel.

His groan vibrates against me, a low, wrecked sound that lights every nerve, every inch of me, on fire.

His hands drift lower, dragging along my ribs, over my stomach, fingertips leaving a trail of fire in their wake. He moves, savoring every sound he pulls from me, every tremor of my body beneath him.

He makes me feel like I'm something rare. Precious.

"Alex," I gasp, my nails digging into his back. "Please."

His breath hitches, and then he meets my gaze. Pupils are blown wide, his expression shifting, restraint slipping just enough to let me see it.

He needs this as much as I do.

He shifts lower, pressing kisses down my stomach, his fingers tracing the waistband of my leggings before tugging them down my hips, my panties with them.

My pulse thunders, heat licking up my spine as he peels them off, leaving me bare beneath him.

His gaze drags over me, dark and reverent, making me feel exposed. Wanted. Seen in a way I never have before.

"Fuck," he mutters, swallowing hard. "You're beautiful."

He kisses his way down my body. I can't help but be self-conscious, but he doesn't let me.

He makes me mindless. His mouth, his hands, never-ending caresses. He crawls down my body, using his hands to spread my legs.

His eyes meet mine, the position compromising, intimate. But the desire, the pure unadulterated need in his eyes, makes my heart stutter. Then he leans down and runs his tongue over my clit, causing me to jump.

Holy shit.

But I don't have time to think about it. Because his mouth, his tongue, his hands, are everywhere. Bringing about pleasure I never even knew was possible. His name is a silent prayer on my lips as he makes me come, my back arching off the bed. My hands grasp his head, wanting to push him away and pull him closer simultaneously. He kisses the inside of my thigh as I catch my breath.

He kisses his way back up my body, swirling his tongue over my breasts, rising over me, with a confident, lazy smirk that tells me he enjoyed that as much as I did.

But I can't help but notice. He's overdressed.

Growing more confident, I grab his shirt and drag him down, pouring all my needs into the kiss, as I use my other hand to fumble at his waistband, desperate to have his skin against mine.

He takes over, undoing his pants, stripping off the rest of his clothes. He lowers himself back down. Our bodies align. Chest to chest. Skin to skin.

Heat spreads like wildfire between us, and something deep inside me cracks open.

I kiss him again, fiercer this time, wrapping my legs around his waist. He groans into my mouth, his control splintering.

"Tell me you're sure," he whispers against my lips, his voice raw, nearly breaking.

I cup his face, forcing him to see me. "I've never been surer of anything."

Whatever restraint he has left snaps.

He kisses me, stealing the air from my lungs, drowning me in sensation as he gives me what we've both been craving.

When he enters me, I gasp—my whole body burning, trembling, overwhelmed by the stretch, the heat of him, the way he whispers my name, needy and desperate.

He stills, his forehead pressed to mine, his breath ragged. "Are you okay?"

I nod, gripping his arms and anchoring myself to him. "Yeah. More than okay."

His mouth curves into a small, knowing smile before he moves again, slow, deliberate, letting me adjust, and feel every inch of him.

We find a rhythm, a perfect, desperate push and pull. A dance that's only ours. Every measured thrust, every stolen kiss, every whispered word sends me spiraling further, pulling me under.

His body molds to mine, every thrust paired with a look, a kiss, a touch that makes me feel impossibly seen.

This isn't just a need.

It's us. The quiet ache we've carried for so long bursts forth.

The pleasure builds, my body tightens, and my shields slip again, emotions bleeding out, wrapping around him, tethering me to him in a way that feels hopeful and terrifying.

Alex groans, his grip tightening on me. "Andy."

"I know."

But when I fall apart beneath him, he follows moments later, his body shaking against mine. I don't care if the whole damn building feels it.

Because this?

This was worth every second of waiting.

TWENTY

Alex

Andy is curled against me, her head resting on my chest, her breathing slow and steady as she dozes. My arm drapes around her, my fingers tracing lazy patterns along the curve of her bare back, memorizing the softness of her skin. Her body fits against mine perfectly. Where she belongs.

I don't want to move; I don't want to lose this moment.

For the first time, nothing is standing between us. No rules, no barriers, no politics dictating who we can or can't be to each other.

It's just us.

I exhale, pressing a slow kiss to the top of her head, letting the weight of everything that's happened settle over me.

This changes things.

Not just for me, not just for Andy, but for everyone.

Because now that I've had her, now that she's here in my arms, mine in every sense of the word, there's no going back.

In the back of my mind, I've always known I loved her. That wasn't a revelation. I'd been falling for Andy since the moment she crashed into my life, stubborn and sharp, with fire in her eyes and something untamed beneath the surface. I was just afraid to admit it. But tonight?

Tonight, something shifted. Something deeper than love.

The word filters through my mind, unbidden yet undeniable.

Mate.

It didn't slam into me—it settled. Solid. Unshakeable. But now, there's no doubt. She's mine.

Mates, it's a theory originally out of Dmitri's camp, but I've read about it. Mason tried to talk to me about it a while ago.

It's a term used in the dockets that Mason has submitted. Bonds and connections, pulls, and the impact of others. Not just family, but now something else. It isn't discussed, not that anything Mason submits is. But it's there.

Now I know it wasn't just an idea; it's a fact.

Andy's my mate. She was always the one person who was my other half.

I just hadn't been able to claim her. Not until now.

The pull we felt for so many years, my inability to walk away, were all caused by this connection that I ignored.

It was staring me in the face, but my pride and inability to bend kept us apart far longer than we should have been.

A surge of protectiveness tightens my chest. I hold her closer, my hand on her back, feeling each steady breath.

I want to keep her here.

Shield her from all the bullshit, from every fight that's still ahead of us. From the inevitable fallout that will come. And there will be fallout. Nothing changes without consequences.

But I don't care. I'll handle whatever comes.

I'll build everything around her, if that's what it takes. Make sure we have the future she wants, where she doesn't have to keep running or fight for space in a world constantly trying to control her.

A future where she's not just mine, but free to be herself.

Andy shifts, her leg sliding over mine, pressing closer.

My breath catches as heat licks up my spine, already too aware of her warmth, scent, and the way she sighs softly against my skin.

Fuck. She's exhausted, but even in the haze of sleep, she clings to me. As if some part of her already knew what I only just realized, what I felt when she collapsed in my arms.

Her breathing changes and I feel her stir, the way her fingers twitch against my chest before her head tilts, her lips grazing my skin.

I inhale sharply, my entire body responding in an instant, a slow pulse of want unfurling in my stomach.

Andy lets out a small sound, half sigh, half sleepy hum as she shifts again, her thigh brushing against me, her skin warm and soft against mine.

I groan, tightening my grip on her waist as I fight for control.

Then she moves again, pressing closer, her lips trailing absentminded kisses along my collarbone, up the curve of my neck, her fingers tracing light patterns over my stomach.

"You're playing a dangerous game," I murmur, my voice rough and low.

Andy blinks up at me, eyes still heavy with sleep, but the look she gives me. Sexy confidence with a dash of mischief.

A slow smile tugs at her lips. She shifts again, straddling me, her hands braced on my chest, her sunshine hair tumbling around her shoulders.

I swallow hard, my fingers flexing against her hips, my control splintering all over again.

"What if I want to play?" she murmurs, her voice still thick with sleep, but undeniably teasing.

I can't stop myself, gripping her waist, flipping us so she's beneath me again, and she gasps, her hands sliding up my arms, her body arching into mine.

My gaze locks onto hers, searching for any hesitation, any uncertainty.

There's none. Only warmth. Only us.

I kiss her again, slower this time, savoring the feel of her lips, the way she sighs into my mouth, the way her body responds to mine.

She's growing bolder, confident. And fuck, it's the most beautiful thing I've ever seen—this unraveling, this surrender, this trust.

I take my time exploring her, letting my hands map her curves, my lips tracing the same path, memorizing every breathy sound she makes, every shift of her hips, every whispered plea.

We move together, no nerves this time, only want—deep and consuming.

I sink into her, and she takes me, her body molding to mine, welcoming me like she was made for this, for me.

And I know without any doubt she was.

She trembles beneath me, her fingers threading through my hair, her breath uneven as she clings to me.

Our kiss turns deeper, slower. I want her to feel it; to know this is more than just pleasure, more than just sex.

This is everything.

I move in a steady rhythm, drawing it out, letting every touch, every press of our bodies build into something more.

Her shields crack again, emotions bleeding out between us. I don't care.

Let them feel it.

Let them all know she's mine.

Her breathing turns ragged, her grip grows more desperate, her body tightens, and then she shatters, writhing beneath me, her soft cries muffled against my shoulder as she falls apart.

I follow her, moaning her name, my body shaking with the sheer force of it, the sheer rightness of it.

When I collapse beside her, pulling her against me, kissing her lightly.

My heartbeat is still unsteady.

Andy sighs, nuzzling closer. "You know, I could get used to this."

I smirk, tightening my hold on her. "Good. Because I'm never letting you go."

She laughs, but I mean it.

Now, nothing can take her from me.

Andy

His heartbeat still thuds beneath my cheek, slower now, steadier, but not calm.

Mine's not either.

His skin is warm against mine; the room is dim and quiet. The only light is the faint glow from the moon filtering through the cracked blinds, painting soft lines across his bare chest, and his jaw, his arm around me like he never intends to let go.

And maybe he won't.

The thought sends a ripple through me. Whatever this is, whatever we have become. It's what I have always hoped for.

Mason was right.

Maybe Fate isn't as much of a fairy tale as I used to tell myself it was.

My body still hums with the memory of us, the way he moved, the way he looked at me.

Like I was something to be cherished. I was something he'd been waiting for.

He made me feel beautiful. Wanted. Seen.

I've never felt this way before, not like this. Not without second-guessing every part of me. Not without the weight of doubt whispering that I wasn't enough.

But last night, I didn't have to perform.

I didn't have to be bold, reckless, or clever. I didn't have to wear confidence-like armor. I just had to be me.

And he met me there with everything he had.

I can still hear the whisper as he said my name, how he moved with so much care and control. Like he never wanted to break me but still needed to claim every part of me.

And I let him. Not because I had something to prove, but because I stopped running from the truth.

I love him.

There is no denying it now.

Not after he made me feel like I was his entire world, like nothing else outside this bed, this room, even existed.

I close my eyes, burying my face in his shoulder, breathing him in.

This is Alex Clarke—my Alex Clarke.

Elitus' golden boy. Rule-follower. Strategist. Reluctant leader. In control, choosing to do the right thing.

He chose me.

Even when he wasn't supposed to. Even when the rules told him not to.

I don't know what strings he had to pull behind the scenes to make this even possible—but when he said he wouldn't have risked it for anyone else. Only me.

It's overwhelming.

And yet... it feels like breathing. Something inside me has clicked into place.

For all my bluster, all my teasing and taunting, I think I've been terrified the whole time.

Terrified, I wasn't enough. That I'd never measure up.

Not up to expectations.

Not to the other girls.

Not to the future I thought he wanted.

But tonight proved I didn't have to be anyone else.

I just had to be his. I lift my head just enough to see him.

He's already watching me, eyes half-lidded but alert, one hand resting on my hip, his thumb tracing circles. A slow smile curves across my lips. "What?" I whisper, brushing my fingers across the sharp line of his jaw.

He shrugs, but there's a softness in his eyes I rarely see. "Just memorizing this."

"This?" I echo.

"You. Here. Like this, safe. Mine."

My heart stutters, a traitorous, too-loud thud that I'm sure he feels.

"You really mean that," I whisper, though it's not quite a question.

He shifts onto his side, sliding his hand beneath my chin, tilting my face toward his thumb, brushing my cheek, his gaze steady, reverent. "I've never meant anything more."

I swallow hard, blinking back the sudden sting behind my eyes.

"Okay," I whisper, voice shaky but certain.

He pulls me closer, lips brushing my forehead. "Go back to sleep. I've got you."

And somehow, I believe him. I let my walls fall without fear.

Because I'm his and he's mine.

And this?

This is just the beginning.

TWENTY-ONE

Alex

The next few days are a goddamn blur.

Between work, committee meetings, and Elitus restructuring; time flies by. But I wouldn't trade it for the world.

Andy's just as swamped finishing her last tests while balancing her role on the residential committee as I am. Kate also convinced her to assist with some other committees. It's working well for her since she hates teaching and lab work.

We get little time for ourselves, but we cherish the brief moments. We celebrated my twenty-second birthday with my family. Small compared to the normal spectacle, but one of the best I've had, especially since Andy was seated next to me during it.

We do our best to balance everything, and although we have had a rough start, our relationship has blossomed. But I can't help but feel like something is looming.

There's a shift in the air. Everything is changing.

Not just for Andy and me, but for everyone.

Our Gen Two class is stepping up, taking on committees, and pushing things forward in ways we never have before.

There's an undercurrent of excitement and anticipation mixed with uncertainty.

People are finally looking toward the future.

Not just the next mission. Not just the next fight. Something more.

I see it in Gen Two, in the way they carry themselves. Stronger. More confident. More aware of their place in this world.

They aren't just soldiers or survivors of the system we were all thrown into. They are becoming leaders.

Andy, especially. She's always been fierce, independent, and unwilling to let anyone dictate her path. But now, standing on the edge of graduation, with everything shifting, she's freer than she's ever been.

And she's mine.

That still hits me sometimes.

After years of dancing around each other, after every near-miss and almost-moment, we've stopped pretending. Now, with no rules hanging over us, we can build something.

Something real.

She spends most nights in my bed, something I didn't expect to happen so naturally.

Maria even took it upon herself to upgrade my bedroom. Modern furniture, a setup for a couple. It was bizarre, but I'm not complaining.

Balancing friendships and a relationship is challenging. But so far? It's working. And we're not the only ones.

Since the dating ban lifted, couples who have spent years avoiding feelings are giving in.

It makes sense. For so long, we couldn't want anything outside duty, survival. Now, people are thinking about their future.

And not just in the romance department.

With the Elitus selections finished, a fresh wave of leadership is rising. I've secured my spot alongside Max, Kate, Reese, Wyatt, and Kyle, a solid mix of Gen One, Two, and Three.

Even McGuire, despite his issues with me pushing the changes, didn't fight it. He could have. He could have kept me out to make a point. But he didn't.

Maybe he realized this was going to happen. We're not kids anymore. This world belongs to us now.

But nothing stands out more than this. As we near the Gen Two graduation, our upper tier of Power Players is expanding. Soon, there will be three X-level classifications.

Kyle. Riddick. Bastian.

Between them, future missions will look different.

More dangerous. More risk. More exposure.

It's not just their power; it's the way they move, and how they lead.

Kyle is a natural leader with a strategic mind. He's the one they look to in the field. He is always predicting, making calculated choices, cataloging everyone's strength, using it for maximum impact.

Riddick, with his adaptability. His range, strength, and innate ability to take control, make split-second adjustments, and tilt the field in our favor.

And Bastian.

The Mental God. A wildcard.

The one they never expect—the silent killer. He can play both sides, offense and defense; a master of both.

For the first time, it feels like we're not just surviving the old system; we're rewriting it, redefining it.

Elitus isn't just a political or military concept anymore. It's becoming what it was always meant to be: a coordinated special unit of super soldiers.

Within it, a command structure for Wights.

We're the ones in the field who know what is needed.

And now? We have a seat at the table.

With them on the field and Wight Elitus on the board; things will change.

Make our world, their world, a little safer for everyone.

But even with all of that; Kyle, Riddick, Bastian, the new structure, the future laid out in front of us, Andy is still the thing that centers me.

She's the one thing that cuts through politics, strategy, the endless games of control and posturing.

With her, it's never been about roles or rank or power.

She doesn't care that I'm on the board now. Andy doesn't give a shit about titles or status, or the fact that McGuire finally stopped fighting me.

She never has.

She cares about the mission, about the people, and about me.

And God, after everything ...

After years of pretending, holding back, and drawing lines that we both kept crossing anyway, she's still the one person who makes me forget about the fight long enough to breathe.

She's my reminder that this world we're trying to build must be about more than duty and sacrifice. It must be about people like her.

People who've spent too long carrying the weight of everyone else's expectations.

People who deserve more than the scraps of what's left after the fighting's done.

Andy's part of that future.

Mine, ours. And yes, I might be the one helping rewrite the rules, reshaping Elitus from the inside, but she's the one rewriting me.

Although I want to protect her from what's coming. I know better.

I know Andy Parrish doesn't need someone to shield her.

She needs someone who'll stand beside her and fight with her, no matter how ugly it gets.

And that's exactly what I intend to do.

Andy

I should have known this was coming.

Roarke told me we were going to dinner at home, and my stomach twisted. A dull unease settled under my skin like a warning. Roarke had said he handled this. I thought we were past it. But the second I step into our father's perfectly arranged dining room, I realize I was mistaken.

The air is thick with tension, the kind that doesn't just hang. It crushes.

The long dining table is meticulously set, with every piece of silverware gleaming, every plate perfectly placed. My mother stands near the head of the table, her hands folded in front of her, her expression unreadable.

My father, Kurt, is sitting and waiting.

Not just for me. For all of us.

Delilah and Ava are already sitting, their postures are ramrod straight, their eyes darting between our parents, and Roarke and I. Delilah clutches her napkin, her knuckles white, while Ava stares at her plate, almost as if she thinks if she doesn't make eye contact, he won't see her.

I hate they have to see this. I hate that I haven't been able to get them out of here.

Roarke stands stiffly beside me, shoulders squared, fists clenched at his sides. He didn't tell me it was this bad.

"Sit."

My father's voice is crisp and clipped, an order.

I don't move right away. I refuse to be commanded like a soldier under his control. But my mother flicks her gaze toward me, something fleeting in her expression. She stands frozen, face blank, but her knuckles are clasped tightly together, a little too tight. Roarke nudges me forward, silently urging me not to fight. Not yet.

So, I sit.

The silence stretches. Thick. Suffocating. Until my father speaks.

"I told you this was over."

I exhale sharply, already so damn tired of this. This has been the same argument for the last several years. "And I told you; I live there. I'm not leaving the dorms."

His jaw tightens, knuckles whitening at the armrest. "Yes. You are."

I lean back, crossing my arms, forcing my voice to stay level. "You don't get to decide that."

"You are my daughter," he snaps. "And I will not allow you to continue down this path, surrounded by them."

That single word drips with disdain. My stomach turns to stone.

Them. Wights. X program operatives. As if we aren't ones ourselves.

Roarke inhales beside me, but I don't hold back. "Say what you really mean, Dad."

His nostrils flare. "You are not one of them, Andrea."

I see red. "We are X," I snap. "Roarke and I were born this way. You hate it, but you did this. You made us—"

His fist slams against the table, rattling the silverware. Delilah flinches, and Ava lets out the smallest, barely audible gasp.

The room falls into dead silence, the echo of his outburst vibrating in my ribs.

His glare sharpens, lips curling into something cruel. "You will not return to the dorms. You will not be a part of their world anymore. And you will not—" his voice drops to something cold and final, "—associate with that Wight ever again."

My chest constricts. This is about Alex.

It's always about Alex. My father was never part of Elitus, although he aspired to be. Kurt hates what they stand for, and his own inadequacies. He holds a grudge, especially towards Robert.

I grit my teeth, my nails digging into my palms beneath the table. "And if I do?"

My father leans forward, his presence overwhelming. "Then you will lose everything."

I keep my face neutral, even as my heart hammers against my ribs. "You already disowned me, remember?" I remind him; my voice is sharper now. Long ago, he declared I was unworthy, especially when I wouldn't follow his commands any longer. Basically, it made me an outcast in my family. "What else do you have to take?"

His eyes gleam with something calculated. "Oh, Andrea. So much more than you think."

The room tilts. "I'll pull your sisters from the program," he says smoothly. "They aren't in combat. Elitus won't stop me. I will remove them from all of it. If this world is so dangerous, so volatile, then perhaps it's time I ensure Delilah and Ava never take another step in it."

Ava's head snaps up, her eyes wide with fear. Delilah's chair creaks as she stiffens, her breaths shallow.

"You can't," I whisper. "They—"

"I can," he cuts me off, his voice like steel. "You think you're so independent? You can make your own choices. That's fine. But don't think for a second that those choices won't come with consequences." He leans back, his expression smoothing into something composed, as if he's already won. "You will move back home. You will listen to me. And if you step foot in that dorm again, your mother and I will be gone. We will leave the program. Your sisters will have no training, no access, no future in the X-world." His voice turns mocking. "And I know you wouldn't want that."

I feel Ava's gaze on me—pleading, terrified.

Delilah's fists tighten, but she doesn't speak.

The world outside of Elitus isn't something that is talked about. Even with their non-combat skills, they would be outsiders, loners. Once you walk away, you cut all ties. And that's assuming Elitus doesn't eliminate them.

I glance at my mother, but she stands there, unmoving.

Silent, letting him dictate our lives.

Roarke snaps, his patience cracking wide open. "You're out of your fucking mind," he growls, his chair scraping loudly as he stands. "You can't keep doing this. Controlling us. Controlling her."

My father doesn't flinch. "Sit down, Roarke."

Roarke glares. "I—"

"Sit."

His voice is sharp as a blade. For a split second, something flickers across Roarke's face. Defeat.

Because we both know this isn't a bluff.

If my father wants them out of this world, he will do it. And what does that mean for them? I don't know. No one has left this late in the game. The only ones who left abandoned their kids or joined the PPG.

And right now? I have no power to stop him.

Roarke sinks back down, jaw locked, fury simmering.

I swallow back the bile rising in my throat, my entire body trembling. "You can't keep us here forever."

My father smiles. "No. But I can keep you long enough to remind you where you belong."

I clench my teeth, forcing my breath to stay even.

I can't win tonight. But this? It's not over.

I push my chair back, stand, my hands shaking. "Then excuse me," I bite out. "Since I have no other options, I'd like to go to my room now."

There's a long pause before my father gives me a mocking nod. "Of course."

I don't wait for anything else. I turn and leave, my heart hammering, my entire body burning with frustration, anger, and something worse.

Despair.

I shut the door behind me. I hear Roarke's voice from the dining room—low, urgent, and desperate.

I don't hear my father's response.

But I already know.

Roarke will leave.

I won't.

It's time Roarke stopped handling this in silence. It's beyond time for him to take this to Elitus.

Because if Alex and his father get involved, if they push back, maybe I can get out, get my sisters out.

And maybe... I can even save her.

The mother who let this happen. The woman who stood in silence while our father dictated our misery.

TWENTY-TWO

Alex

I'm buried in documents when my phone rings. Andy's name flashes across the screen, and my stomach drops.

Roarke and Andy went home for dinner, and while she tried to play it off, I saw the panic in her eyes before she left. She wouldn't tell me why, but it was enough to put me on edge.

Now, seeing her name on my phone only makes it worse.

I respond at once. "Andy?"

Before she even says anything, I feel her. The raw, electric pulse of her anger and pain bleeds through the line—thick and heavy, pressing against my skin.

"He banned me from the dorms!" she yells, her voice furious.

Angry Andy isn't new to me. I know how she burns, how her fire can consume everything in its path.

But this? This is different. "He can't do this," she snaps.

In the background, I hear Delilah murmuring, trying to calm her down, but Andy is too far gone, spiraling in frustration.

"Where's Roarke?" I ask, already running scenarios.

"Headed back to the dorms," she mutters. "He tried to argue, but it didn't go well. He said he'll be back soon." A sharp inhale. "He's a fucking asshole." She doesn't have to clarify whom.

I drag a hand through my hair, forcing myself to stay calm—for her. "Do you want me to come over there?"

"No," she blurts. But I catch Delilah's voice in the background, telling her it's not a good idea.

Andy ignores her. "I'll wait for Roarke before I call in backup. Mya's coming over with Aimee. He flipped out on De, too. Poor Ava was crying, Alex. He threatened to pull them from the program! I fucking hate him."

That sends a fresh wave of anger through me. My grip tightens on the phone.

"I know," I say, forcing my own emotions down. "Let me talk to Roarke. If I need to involve my father, I will. You're almost twenty-one, nearly graduated, Andy. You're an adult. He has no legal right to keep you there."

"He never gives a shit any other time, now—now he wants to act like he cares?"

"Andy," my voice softens, grounding her. "Take a deep breath. Sit down. Wait for Mya. Let Roarke and me handle this. Don't do anything—"

"Stupid?"

I smirk despite myself. "No liquid courage required this time."

She lets out a sound—part hiccup, part sob—and it wrecks me.

"Alex," she whispers, and I hear everything in that one word.

"I know," I murmur, pressing my fingers against my forehead, aching to reach through the phone and hold her. "Don't worry. I'll fix this. Trust me, Andy."

I keep talking to her, reassuring her, keeping her from tipping over the edge until I hang up.

But I don't waste a second. I call Aimee and Mya, giving them the rundown, ensuring someone is aware, and can work to keep things in control until Roarke and I sort it out.

Then I head downstairs, looking for Roarke. When I reach his room, I see Mason standing in the doorway, arms crossed.

The second Roarke sees me; I don't bother hiding my anger. "What the fuck, Roarke?" I demand.

He's standing near his desk; hands braced against the surface like he's barely holding himself together. His shoulders are tense, jaw locked tight enough to look painful.

"I know," he says, his voice rough but controlled. He doesn't look at me but exhales sharply through his nose before turning toward me. "I'll talk to him."

I step closer, my chest tight. "Andy is losing it right now. I just got off the phone with Mya and Aimee—Delilah is upset, too. They're both heading over there to check on them."

Roarke freezes. For a second, something flickers in his expression—fear.

It's gone as fast as it came, buried under frustration and exhaustion.

But I see it. "Aimee and Mya?" His voice is controlled, but I hear the edge of concern underneath it.

Mason shifts beside me, picking up on the shift, too. "She'll be back," Mason says, trying to sound reassuring. "He can't keep Andy there."

Roarke nods, but there is a tightness in the movement, a stiffness in his posture that wasn't there before.

His father is volatile. That's why he never made it in Elitus. And Mya? She's fearless and doesn't mince words. And she's walking straight into that house, into their father's domain. I don't like it. Neither does Roarke.

But he doesn't say it. He swallows, shakes his head, and mutters, "I'll handle it."

"You better," I snap.

He meets my gaze, and for once, Roarke looks exhausted, not just tired, bone-deep drained.

"This isn't just about Andy," Roarke says, his voice low. "He's losing control, Alex. He's desperate. If he follows through on his threat, if he tries to pull our sisters out of the program..." He trails off, his fingers pressing harder against the desk.

I exhale, pressing my hands to my hips. "Maybe it's time we took it to my father. To Elitus."

He doesn't react, but I see a flicker of consideration in his eyes.

Roarke never wanted Elitus in his home life. He's spent years containing it—containing him—but maybe he's realizing he can't fix this alone.

Realizing that he shouldn't have to.

I don't wait for his answer. I pull out my phone and dial.

My father picks up on the first ring. "Alex?"

I take a breath, steadying myself. "We have a problem."

I don't sugarcoat it. I hold nothing back. I lay out the control, the manipulation, the threats. Roarke's father is trying to rip Andy from the dorms; the only home she's ever had that's safe. That he's threatening to take Delilah and Ava, too.

My father listens in silence, and when I'm done, his voice is sharp.

"Bring Roarke to me," he says. "Now."

I hang up and look at Roarke. He's already grabbing his jacket; there's no hesitation anymore.

Roarke says nothing, but the way he looks, I know. He's done.

This time, he's not protecting their silence. This time, he's breaking it.

Mason's right beside us in this fight. She doesn't say much, but she's already running solutions and working on the angles.

My dad, Roarke, and I discuss options. We are waiting to hear from Mya and Aimee before we move.

Mason looks frustrated, but I know she's keeping a pulse on the Parrish household. When I feel her stiffen, I whip around. Her pupils expand, eerie purple flaring in her irises. Before we can ask what's wrong, she's teleporting out.

I don't have to guess where she's going.

Roarke mutters a curse, his whole body vibrating with tension.

My father steps into the hallway, already calling Elitus. There's no hesitation.

This isn't just about Andy anymore. It's about Delilah, Ava. Their mother.

This is about stopping it. Roarke and I prepare to go after her.

But before he can pinpoint her location, Mason reappears, bringing reality back with her.

Our sisters, Andy, Delilah, and Ava. All of them.

Andy's shaking, her face streaked with tears, but I can't process it. I watch as Mason inspects Mya and her face. She is cradling her cheek, a welt blooming there.

What the fuck.

Every muscle coils tight, my skin itching to shift. It takes everything in me to hold it back, to keep from losing control right here in the damn living room.

I hear Mya give Mason a quick recap. Aggravated that she let her guard down around him, being Mya's biggest complaint.

I haven't asked yet. I can't.

Instead, I focus on Andy, pulling her against me, holding her close. "It's okay," I murmur.

Roarke steps forward, voice cold, direct. "Has he touched Mom?"

Andy doesn't answer. Roarke's jaw clenches. "Has he hit you?"

She exhales. "Don't. It doesn't matter."

"Fuck that," Roarke snaps. "Why didn't you tell me?"

Andy's shoulders shake, her hands curling into fists against my chest. "I should've told you, Roarke. She made me cover for her. She begged me too. He's been abusing her. I tried to step in, but—" she gestures at Mya's face, her voice breaking.

Roarke's breathing turns sharp and uneven. His hands clench at his sides, his entire body radiating something dark and dangerous.

His anger isn't loud. It's not explosive.

It simmers. Hot. The kind that destroys.

If he was done before, he is beyond done now.

We exchange a look, and in that single glance, we both know.

This ends tonight.

I nod to him, and without hesitation, Roarke teleports us both straight to his parents' house.

TWENTY-THREE

Alex

I don't even try to hold back my shift this time. My skin hums with the need for violence, my body itching for the fight.

Roarke is the same. His steps measured as we stalked toward the house, up the front steps.

Every step is precise and purposeful.

This isn't the diplomatic Roarke. This is the Roarke who burns things down. He will take the lead, but we both are determined to ensure things change. I don't know what Andy has gone through, but whatever it is, I am now beginning to understand more some reasons for her acting out all these years. And I hate that I didn't pick up on it. I didn't see it.

Inside, his mother, Jackie, looks up from the kitchen as we enter, her face pale with exhaustion. Roarke's voice is hard as steel. "Mom, you need to leave."

She blinks, assessing her son. Who looks like he is one inch away from committing a capital crime. "Roarke, he is your father."

"Really?" Roarke's laugh is sharp, humorless. "My father would never strike a girl. That cokehead over there? Yeah, he might." His eyes flick toward the lit hallway, where Kurt stands, looking dazed, pupils wide.

"Mom, this ends tonight. I won't let this be the life for my sisters anymore."

His dad laughs, muttering to himself. Kurt has always had a temper, and a general lack of control. He barely attends any Elitus events, which, based upon what I am seeing, is by design. Jackie still isn't budging, whether she is in shock or denial or both.

"Alex would be more than happy to gut you for what you did to Andy," Roarke says, voice ice-cold, as he speaks to his father. "And I wouldn't blame him. If I'd known, you'd already be dead. You can leave now, or you can stay and die. Your choice. I don't play games with my family."

His face twists into something cruel. "This is my fucking family. Not yours. All of you are nothing. Mistakes. Big fucking mistakes." Kurt's gaze swings to his wife. "Jackie, let's go."

She stands on shaking legs, but Roarke moves faster, stepping in front of her, cutting off his chance to touch her. Roarke looks at his mother, communicating more with his eyes than with his words. Whatever she sees makes her pause.

Jackie looks at her husband, resigned. "Kurt, just leave," she begs, her voice breaking. "Please."

His lips curl back. "You would stay here? With them?"

Her chin trembles, but her voice is steady. "They're my children. Our children. Of course, I would. I love them."

He scoffs pure venom in his voice. "They're all going to leave you. To go fuck someone else. Make more fucking mutants. Now, Jackie. Roarke, move."

"No, she stays."

He nudges his mom back, fixing his gaze on his father. I see Kurt's body twitch, the shifty dart of his eyes. He's high, unpredictable and desperate. And he's fucking stupid.

Roarke and his dad have the same build, tall and broad, but Roarke is stronger. After hearing everything, it's obvious his strength wasn't just for the field. But for home as well. Deep down, he must've known it would end like this.

When Kurt decides and gets ready to fight, he stares at us, then laughs—a sick laugh, something hollow and broken.

Then he lunges at me. I'm not surprised, but I don't have time to react.

Roarke knew what he was going to do. It's like he has been waiting for this. He steps in front of me.

Kurt isn't prepared for the sheer power and strength of Roarke.

Roarke dodges the first hit, and Kurt tries to counter and strike back again. But misses, and Roarke counters with brutal precision. He doesn't fight to maim—he fights to end this.

Every punch is calculated, and every movement precise. It doesn't take long before Kurt is on the floor, wheezing, clutching his ribs.

Roarke crouches over him, voice lethal. "Leave. You aren't welcome here. If you come back, I'll kill you myself."

My fists tighten as my power hums under my skin, begging for release. "We aren't mutants or mistakes—we are the future. You're the mistake. You had everything—a wife who loved you, three daughters who needed you. And you threw it all away. That's on you. Not us."

Behind us, Riddick, Stephen, and Ace enter. Security floods in after. My father stands with them, his face unreadable. But his presence? Unshakable.

He listens, I explain what happened, and inform him of everything we missed over the years.

The guilt settles like a stone in my chest.

He feels it too; I see it in his expression. We should have known. We should have seen this coming.

But Robert doesn't waste time on regrets. He looks at Jackie. He is done with sitting back.

His voice is final. "She's coming with us."

At my dad's, the second I see Andy, I pull her into me, into my arms.

She collapses onto my chest.

My father steps forward, placing a hand on her back—silent comfort.

Security is managing the rest at the Parrish house. Andy sniffles against my shirt, voice small as she asks, "We're staying here?"

I nod, kissing her hair. "Yeah, for now." She shudders, her grip tightening on me. I kiss her, sending her upstairs to settle her sisters and mom for the night.

It took some convincing, but Roarke finally talked Jackie into leaving for the night.

He comes down after settling his mom into a room. His face is unreadable, his shoulders sagging with exhaustion. "We're staying here tonight," I tell him.

"Good." His voice is hoarse. "I need to hit the dorms. I can't... I can't be here right now." I nod and take a step forward.

"Do you need to talk about it?" I ask.

"Alex, this day has been long overdue. I feel nothing other than relief right now. Just monitor my mom and the girls. I have to get some air," with a sad smile, he leaves. Porting out to regroup with Riddick and security while I head upstairs.

Andy is curled up with Delilah and Ava, whispering to them. But the second she sees me; she stands and wraps herself around me.

It sinks in that I almost lost her today. It hits me hard, what she has gone through. They have all gone through.

It explains a lot about her behavior, her need for control. I hate how she has suffered. I lift her, carrying her to bed. She doesn't fight me.

She buries herself against me, and I hold her.

Promising myself that no one will ever take her from me again.

Andy

The next morning, I wake up feeling like a freight train has hit me.

Not physically, though the exhaustion sits heavy in my bones. But emotionally, mentally.

A tiredness that goes deeper. The kind that makes you want to crawl under the covers and shut the world out.

But I can't. Roarke comes by in the morning. He spends a decent amount of time trying to talk to Mom, leaving me to deal with De and Ava. It's fine. It's normal, in a way that isn't.

Everything is different now. And yet... all I feel is relief.

Not joy, nor triumph. Just that deep exhale after holding your breath for years without realizing it. I keep waiting for the guilt to follow. Waiting for the panic or regret. But it doesn't come. Not yet anyway.

Mason checks in, so do Aimee and Mya. All the girls. Alex is close, hovering without crowding, helping smooth things out with Elitus, deflecting any outside drama like a shield I didn't ask for but desperately needed.

Roarke updates me on where we are going from here, what the plan is. As much as I hate it, De and Ava will return home with Mom. I know De in the new year hopes to get out. But Ava, she is quiet and shy. As part of Gen Five, her powers are less than ours. She will not go into combat, but she does well in schooling. However, I see it in her eyes. The worry, she is so young to be dealing with something this heavy.

Roarke and I will both spend more time at home now. Try to repair the wounds left behind. But also, to keep a close eye on our mother, who spent decades shrinking under a man who believes silence was obedience and bruises were correction. Those scars run deep, and I don't know who she'll be without him. I don't know who I will be.

Alex joins us for lunch and informs me that his moms have been busy.

I guess after hearing about it, Maria along with her mommy squad have decided that they want to remove all remnants of Kurt from our family home.

What that means, I am not entirely sure, but knowing Maria, it's over the top, and sure to make my sisters happy at least. And that's all I can ask for. After lunch, Aimee, Mya, Rina and Ariel all come by to hang out with my sisters. I sneak back to the dorms. Alex has given me space, but he has also been more supportive than I could've asked for.

I know he feels guilty, like he should've known. Should've seen the signs. I tried to explain that Roarke was good at hiding and covering for our dad. That we didn't want Elitus interference. Mostly, we handled it. We did what we could to get out of there, and to keep our sisters as safe as they could be.

I'm struggling to deal with my feelings. I have avoided them for so long, and there has been so much change in everything, not just last night, but in the last two weeks. Alex has been quiet, supportive, and a good listener.

I don't know how much longer I can hold all this inside. I'm afraid of what this all means.

Roarke needs to talk as well, but he has been silent and focused. Taking care of financial things for Mom, removing my father from any paperwork that needs to happen. I am too afraid to ask what happened to our dad. Where he is. So, I pretend like I am indifferent. But I am sure Alex sees right through me.

Alex

Andy has been lost in her own head today. I understand it; she went through the motions, helping her sisters, working with Roarke, talking to friends, but in her head. I know she has a whirlwind going.

It eats me up inside to know that this has been going on. Well, to this extent, anyway. I am thankful Roarke got her out of that house. This morning, I left Andy sleeping in my bed and spent some time with Roarke. I wanted to know what I was dealing with when it came to verbal abuse, and possibly physical. He didn't hold back, laid it all out. And what I heard made me want to hunt Kurt down and hurt him. How Roarke didn't kill him, I don't know.

I also don't miss the tension in Roarke, and this whole situation. The burden he has carried. Riddick and I both agreed to help as much as we can, as well mentally Roarke is going to need to offload. He was already having issues prior to this blowout. Now, he's going to need an outlet.

My moms took on the added task of some renovations to the Parrish household. It's amazing what those women can do. They have an entire army of contractors at the house. Painting, revamping it. Dad has already said that Jackie and the girls can stay as long as they like. I let Andy know we can stay at my parents' or the dorms. Whatever she preferred.

Even with all this drama, work doesn't stop. Mission contracts and new housing plans keep my calendar busy. With a light knock on my dorm door, it opens quietly. And there she is.

"Hey," I say, trying to give her a warm smile. She looks a little lost, a little depressed. And I want to kick my own ass. To think I added to her drama for the last year because I was an idiot and didn't have the guts to push for change. That she was dealing with all of this, and that I could've been a support for her.

Instead, even though not my intention, I know my back and forth, my inability to make her a priority, had hurt her. I am thankful she never gave up hope for me.

I hate that both she and Roarke were in that situation. Dealing with the constant narcissistic behavior and mental abuse from their father. Trying to protect their sisters when they had little control.

I stand and open my arms, and Andy comes to me without hesitation.

And she holds on. I kiss her head, breathing her in. I want to be her safe space, to be the one she can go to when she needs to talk. Or for whatever she needs.

"I had to take a break," she tells me quietly.

"That's okay. Mya will let us know if they need anything." I know Mya has been helping all the girls and has agreed to stay at home until De and the rest go back to their parent's house. Aimee is there as well. That means Mom is cooking up a storm, so our house will be the prime spot to be at tonight. Whenever Joanne cooks, our house becomes an open door. I know without a doubt, unless I tell them otherwise, all our friends will be by. Showing support, trying to take everyone's mind off of it. I am thankful for that. We are lucky to have built a friendship and a family with our fellow Wights.

I look down at her. "What do you need?" She says nothing, just hugs me harder. It took a long time for her to fall asleep last night. She didn't want to talk about it, but she was restless. She isn't in training right now. I'm not concerned about any of that. Riddick has covered Roarke's missions for the week. Trials and graduation will come, but Andy and Roarke's rankings are solid.

Roarke has always been a powerhouse in Threes. Both the physical aspect and his ability to bend time and space, the porting and his use of his ones in conjunction to make him a shield for Mason and others. He will never hit X, but his status as a High Three is solid.

Andy, she has never really pursued anything outside of her ability to port. Mason has always worked with her, and she is more than able to defend and fight. But she hates it, even if she won't admit it. That's why her job is usually transport, scouting, and retrieval. She will also declare High, because she is one of the strongest porters we have. Honestly, it's one of the most useful abilities. I don't want to even think about her in combat right now, so instead I concentrate on making her feel better.

I grab her hand and lead her over to my bed. I lie down and pull her down with me. A simple gesture, but she rests her head on my chest, wrapping herself around me. I brush my hand over her head, her hair, and down her back. A soothing motion. One I remember my mom doing whenever I was upset about something or another.

She sighs into me. She hasn't cried yet. Or screamed. Or been Angry Andy. I know she will eventually. It's coming. But for now, I will just wait it out with her.

TWENTY-FOUR

Andy

Tomorrow, my family is moving back to our home. It's been a couple of days, and it's finally finished. It's been nearly a week since the blowout, and Alex and I have been at Robert and Maria's a lot.

Alex and I had spent every night with his parents, but tonight I told him I wanted to go back to the dorms. I can never thank them enough for the love and support of my mom and sisters.

Maria opened their home not only to our family, but to our friends, who were a steady stream of support. It was a pleasant distraction, and although my mother was quiet in the corner, it had been a long time since she could see all her children relaxed and smiling.

Leaving tonight, I could've sworn I caught a small smile on her face when I hugged her and said goodnight. If so, I hope she realizes she is still her own person.

I found some books and information on recovery after domestic abuse. I ordered them; I don't know if she will read them, but I am hopeful.

Alex opens the door of his BMW. His parents' house is about a mile and a half from the dorms, and I could port, but I know Alex likes to drive. An idea pops into my head, and I can't help but blurt it out.

"Can we go off campus? For just a ride?"

He side-eyes me as he starts the car. The steady purr of the engine. I know it's risky, but I need to get out. Somewhere else, breathe a little. He hits the phone and calls his father.

"Yes," Robert answers on the first ring.

"I'm going to take Andy off campus, just for a drive, some air," he tells his father.

"Okay."

"And I'm borrowing the Ferrari," he says with a smirk at me. I don't know what that means, but the gleam in his eye tells me this will be a treat for both of us. Robert is quiet on the other side of the line.

"Don't tell your sister," Alex laughs and hangs up. He drives us around the back of the house, down towards where the enormous hangar and barns are. It's where I know Robert keeps his car collection. Stephen has a helicopter. There is a small Cessna that gets used for McGuire occasionally. When Alex drives in, I am in awe. I have heard all about the car collection but never seen it.

Getting out, Alex takes my hand. "I figured you wanted to get out and lose yourself a little. Best way to do that is in something that makes you feel like you're in a rocket ship," he says with a smile.

"What did he mean by don't tell your sister?"

"Mason loves driving this car, but she doesn't get to very often. Only when someone else goes with her. And lately, she has been so focused, she hasn't asked. But she will be jealous." He smiles at me. I don't know any of these cars; I haven't been a car girl. But Alex nods to a futuristic-looking sleek thing.

"McLaren Speedtail," he says, regarding it. "And that's an Aston Martin," he points to a blue car, which I think is the car James Bond drives. "Porsche 911." It's bright yellow.

"That's my favorite color," I tell him. He smiles at me and kisses my forehead.

"Dodge Viper," a red car that has an open-roof contraption. "It's called T-Tops," he says at my questioning glance. "These are his nostalgia cars, ones that he wanted or drove when he was younger," Alex gestures to a couple of not so fancy cars. A jeep, a lifted truck, and an '80s-style Camaro. I know that one!

We pass along some more sports cars; I stop in front of one. It's white with blue racing stripes. "Ahh, Eleanor's twin," he says. "'67 Mustang Shelby, my father's baby. Or so Mom says. He loves this car."

"It's beautiful."

"Fast, sleek. Back when American-made cars were awesome. Have you seen Gone in Sixty Seconds?"

"No." I don't watch movies; I don't have time. And the only time I do is with the girls.

"I'll tell Mason to add it to your list. She loves Timothy Olyphant, so she will pull it right up." I smile at him. He gestures to the red sports car, opening my door for me. I slide inside. The leather interior has a certain smell. I buckle my seat belt and look at Alex.

"Can I drive?" I ask. He looks at me.

"Do you know how to drive?" Since we aren't allowed off campus, most of us do not bother with a license. Roarke always drives if we need to get around. And I can port, so it's unnecessary.

"I know the basics," I tell him. He smiles.

"I'll teach you to drive, then you can drive a fast car. For now, sit back and let me show you what she can do."

"She?"

"All cars are girls," he tells me. He starts the car and takes us out and off campus.

Alex

Andy has a smile on her face as I speed along the winding curves that lead off campus. The gatehouse was prepared for me to leave; Dad must have called ahead. I messaged Roarke, letting him know. He said Riddick will keep a cover out in case of issues. There shouldn't be any, but I understand and am all for protection for Andy.

I side-eye her as I shift gears, revving the engine as I go, just to see her reaction. She looks happy.

I head out to an accessible area, one that is a great lookout spot. Mason can read my path from this far, so I let her know where I will be. She will update them, but it'll give Andy and me some alone time.

After about twenty minutes, I end up in a hilltop area. It's probably a local make-out spot for teens, but to me, it's a perfect view of the hillside, and a lake that isn't far off. I always thought it would be a good place to build a house, not too far from campus, but away, outside the world of missions and Elitus. We get out, and she looks out over the horizon. Rolling hills, trees, the lights in the distance. Fresh air, and the only thing you hear is the distant call of the night.

The moon is full tonight, and it casts a glow over us. Andy looks radiant. Her leggings and the tank top she has on hug her. Her shoes, not combat boots today, but simple tennis shoes. The best part of her outfit is my sweatshirt that she is wearing over it all. It is huge on her, but seeing her in it this morning when she came downstairs did something to me. I know there is no going back for us, only forward.

That's why I have been so cautious with her for the last couple of days. Roarke and I are both concerned. She's more withdrawn than normal, and I know she is in her own head. She needs to deal with it. Even if it's beating on someone. Mason and Mya offered to train with her, but she turned them down. Wanted to "take care" of her sisters and Mom.

We stand there, my hand in hers. I watch her as she looks out over the land. She takes a deep breath, and her eyes drift to me. And I see it, the weight she has been carrying, she is still holding it all in.

"Is this better?" I ask her. She turns and smiles at me.

"Yes," she says quietly. "I needed to breathe, and sometimes it's so hard there, with them around." She's quiet as she offloads. I just listen, my hand in hers, my presence hopefully making her feel safe.

She turns and steps into me, letting go of my hand so that she can put her arms around my neck. My hands find her waist, gripping her hips. I search her face, trying to determine what she needs. She drops some shielding for me. We have been working on this.

Over the last week or so, we have worked on her shielding ability. Namely, my ability to cover her. Mason has worked with us to help. Andy sucks at it, so it's a work in progress. But I have learned how to read her, how to allow my power to cover her. And right now, her entire system is in upheaval. But what is the loudest? That she wants to forget, that she wants me to distract her.

I lean down and kiss her. Her fingers grasp the strands of hair at the back of my head, and I feel it when she drops some of the worry. Her mind stops spinning. She can focus on this instead. And I let her.

My need to protect her has only grown since we have been together. The constant worry is always present, but more than that, the connection between us grows with every touch, every whisper. The last couple of days have been a change, but when I think about where we were three weeks ago, to where we are now, it's like a 180-degree turn. And I will do just about anything to keep her in this headspace, where she can focus on us, and let me worry about the rest.

She kisses me back. Not slow, not hesitant, but full of everything she has been feeling. I feel the need arise, and my passion ignites when she lets out a soft, gentle moan. My hands move down from her waist to her ass and lift her easily, turning to place her on the hood. The heat between us only grows. She keeps her legs anchored around my hips as I lean her back. Our kisses are full of heat, promise.

We haven't had nearly the time together intimately as I would like. Life is getting in the way, but this, this feels so right.

Her hands run up and down my back as I cage her in between the hood and my body. "Please," she murmurs. A soft moan escaping her as my lips move down along her jaw, down the curve of her neck, slow and reverent. She tilts her head to the side, offering me more. Her pulse hammers beneath my lips, and my hands slide under the sweatshirt, under her top, taking her nipple between my fingers to pinch lightly. The moan she elicits lights my skin on fire even more.

With our shields intertwined, every pulse is magnified between us. Every need, every caress, is shared within our connection, both mentally and physically. And right now, her need is to lose herself in me.

We are out in the open, and I don't like the exposure, but that doesn't mean I am going to let that stop me from making her come. I yank my sweatshirt off her, balling it up and placing it under her head. She looks at me with heavy-lidded eyes, pleasure and need begging for me in those hazel eyes.

I run my hands over her body, my fingers pulling down the thin straps of her tank top and bra, releasing her breasts to the cool air. Her nipples pebble up from the cold, but not for long. Replacing the cool air with my mouth, Andy arches her back and grasps my head.

I want her so damn bad, but I am not about to fuck her on top of the Ferrari out in the open. Adding shields to my own needs, I adjust; otherwise, my hormones will make me do something stupidly reckless.

I focus on her, the way she moves, the little gasps. She has one hand holding onto my hair, her fingers clasping and unclasping on the hair at my nape. Her other hand encircles the breast I am neglecting.

I adjust my stance, one hand braced over her head against the hood, the other slides down her body, tugging at her leggings, allowing me to get to her. I slide my hands inside; her satin panties are not much of a barrier to her heat, slipping my fingers underneath. She's soaked.

I move my mouth across her chest as she pulls down the rest of her top, allowing me access. I kiss, lick, and nibble. She lets out a small gasp, and my eyes travel up to her face. To watch her. Her head is thrown back, her mouth ajar. She is lost in pleasure as my mouth and fingers bring her higher.

As if she senses me watching her, she tips her head down and our eyes lock. The look she gives me; it takes every ounce of strength and self-control I have not to take her here. Fuck, she's beautiful. Flushed cheeks, her hair a sexy mess. Her eyes are on mine as I pump my fingers in and out of her pussy, my thumb applying the right amount of pressure on that bundle of nerves that makes her eyes roll back.

"Look at me," I murmur, my mouth working her nipple. She catches my gaze. Our eyes locked, the message between us not only with our eyes, but our shared connection through the shields. "Are you going to come for me, beautiful?" I ask her in a quiet tone.

"Only for you," she murmurs, eyes locked with mine. I speed up my fingers. It's taking effort for her not to throw her head back, but she keeps her eyes on me. I blow gently across her nipples, and a ragged moan escapes her as her eyes flick up to the sky and back to me. "Please."

"Come," I murmur against her breast, and she does. Her face is a picture of ecstasy. Her body flutters around my fingers as I slowly bring her back from her high. She collapses back, her eyes still watching me, but her head is against the car and tilted down. Her body is languid and lax.

Lifting my body up, I kiss my way up her chest, her neck, until we are face to face again. I readjust her top and leggings, gently caressing her side. I kiss her nose, and she gives me a soft smile.

"You okay?" I ask. She sighs dramatically, and I can't help but laugh.

"I'm great," she murmurs, leaning up a little to kiss me. "When we get home, you are doing that again," she tells me. This time, with a spark in her eye, I have missed. For now, I will do anything to see that. To let the world go for a bit.

"You sure are a demanding little thing tonight," I tell her. She gives me that sexy smirk that makes me want to show her exactly what I want to do with her demands.

"Are you complaining?" She asks with a lightness in her voice I haven't heard in several days.

"Not at all." I kiss her one more time and pull her up with me. Her skin is flushed, but she grabs my sweatshirt anyway, and I swear she smells it before she throws it over her head.

I smile to myself a little. Thinking about how many more articles of clothing I can leave for her.

I adjust myself and glance at the car quickly. No visible damage. God knows Mason, never mind, my father would have killed me if we scratched it. But it would've been worth it.

TWENTY-FIVE

Andy

After last night, I feel a bit more like me. Alex seems to read me so well. It's almost as if he knows what I am thinking. If he were a stronger Two, I would believe it. Maybe with time, it'll be natural for both of us.

After the adventure in the Ferrari, we made it back in record time to the dorms. And got lost in his bedroom for eight hours. It was delicious, and my body is sore in all the right ways. Alex was gentle but demanding. His body knows just what I need and how I need it.

I stretch out my limbs as I change. We showered earlier, which was just another excuse to have sex. I really like shower sex. Who am I kidding? I like anytime we get to be intimate.

The last few weeks have been a whirlwind, and I only hope it will get back to normal soon. Or whatever normal will be. I appreciate the distraction the last 12 hours have been.

Alex took my mind off it. But I know I need to face reality.

He had been so tender, so comforting, everything I could've asked for in a supportive partner. He hasn't pressed, but I see the concern on his face, on Roarke's. Even Mason and Mya. They aren't pushing, just letting me know they are there if I need to talk. I appreciate it more than they can know.

But I can't break, not right now. If I do, it'll be disastrous. I want to get my sisters settled, and my mom. Get them back into the house. Then maybe I will take some time to sort through my thoughts.

Roarke grabs us from Alex's room. After the first couple of nights Alex and I were together, he requested we never come back to my room. I laughed, but I get it. Mason has been working with us on shielding, but I think that for my twin, it'll always be an issue.

Roarke has his own issues, never mind our family drama. He looks more stressed, not less, which worries me.

"Are you okay?" I ask him. Alex walks with us. His hand in mine. We will go to the Clarkes, then to our home.

"Yea," he says, but his tone doesn't fit with the words. "Let's get them settled," he says, clearly done with the conversation. My eyes catch Alex's, and he nods his head. He will help deal with whatever it is for Roarke, him and Riddick both.

Collecting my sisters and mom, we take them to the house. For my mom, it's the first time she has ported. She looks a little shocked once we land on our doorstep. Looking at both Roarke and me. Maybe she now realizes what that really means.

I mean, she knows; she is aware, but our father kept her so far out of all Elitus' things, because of his own issues, that she never really could celebrate what her children can do. We didn't talk about powers or missions at home. We barely talked. And me?

My relationship with her was already strained when I was younger, due mostly to her not defending me against him.

Over the last several days, I realized what it was. She was protecting us in the only way she knew how. She let herself take the brunt of his anger. Always deflecting when I said something that aggravated him, or De or Ava made a mistake that would cause his temper to go off. Thinking back now, she did a lot of stupid things to draw his attention. And I am sure once he got her alone, he made her pay for it.

With a scowl, I can't hide. We enter the house.

I stop in the entryway and just stare.

This is not the house we grew up in. I'm tempted to step out and check the house number. It's not the place where walls reek of fear and anger; in memories none of us wants.

That place is gone.

Maria, Sarah, and the rest of the mommy squad didn't just remove Kurt from the picture; they erased him. They not only refreshed, repainted but also remodeled. An open floor plan with some beams, give it a more rustic feel. The walls are lighter, and the dining area, which was the principal place where the verbal abuse would take place, has been gutted. And in its place, an archway opens to our kitchen. Fresh paint in the kitchen, a new dining set, which is a contrast from the long formal dining table my father had insisted we sit at.

This remodeled home is a breath of fresh air I didn't know I needed. Walls that once held my father's rage were torn down. Literally. Metaphorically. Rooms, once heavy with tension, are now open. Welcoming. New.

Maria, being Maria, had directed it like a damn military operation. Sarah, Riddick's mom, had worked just as effectively. I heard even the security detail had helped, hauling out every reminder of the man who had spent his life making sure we felt less.

Now, it looks different.

I step into the house, and it feels different. I don't feel his presence.

I should feel relieved, but all I feel is raw.

Everything is too much, too fast, too sudden.

I helped Roarke move our mom and sisters back in. I hug Maria and Sarah, thanking them. Maria tells me she left "a few surprises" in my old bedroom; knowing her, a full wardrobe reset because trauma requires new clothes.

I go through the motions. I function. But the whole time, my mind's stuck.

Now that it's over, I'm unsure what to do with all this rage still sitting in my chest.

Or worse.

The grief.

Because as much as I hate him...

There's still a part of me that wishes he'd been different. Wanted us and loved us the way a father should.

But he didn't. And he never would.

I barely hear Roarke calling my name before Alex appears, his hands on my shoulders, grounding me.

"Andy," he murmurs, searching my face. "Talk to me."

I shake my head. "I don't—" My voice cracks, and I hate it.

His hands tighten, steady. Sure. "Come with me." He doesn't wait for an answer. He moves me with him.

We end up outside, in the backyard. Where it's quiet. Where I can just be.

Alex says nothing at first. He pulls me against his chest, wrapping his arms around me, letting me feel him. And after everything, that's all it takes.

The dam breaks. I don't cry pretty; it's ugly, full-body-shaking sobs that make my chest ache. Alex holds me through it.

His fingers thread through my hair. His voice is low, murmuring against my temple. "It's okay. Let it out. I've got you."

And he does. He holds me together when I'm coming apart at the seams.

"I hate him," I whisper, voice shaking. "I hate him, but—"

Alex doesn't push. He waits. "But part of me..." My breath hitches. "I wish it had been different."

His arms tighten around me.

"I know, Andy."

I squeeze my eyes shut. "I don't want to miss him, Alex."

"You don't," he says. "You're mourning the idea of him. The father you should have had."

I inhale because he's right. I never had a father. Just a man who dictated my life, who controlled me, and made me feel small.

And now that he's gone, I'm not sure how to handle everything I am feeling.

"I feel stupid," I murmur, my face still pressed against his chest.

Alex tilts my chin up. Forcing me to meet his eyes. "Don't say that."

His voice is gentle but firm. "Andy, this is big. What you went through? What your family went through? No one comes out of that without feeling something."

I press my lips together, fresh tears slipping down my cheeks. Alex exhales, brushing his thumb under my eyes. "But you don't have to carry this alone."

I nod, but I couldn't find words, unable to make my mouth work.

And then I don't have to. Alex leans in, pressing his forehead against mine, and says the one thing I didn't realize I needed to hear.

"I love you."

Everything inside me stills.

Stops. His hands cradle my face, his thumbs brushing against my jaw, his breath warm as it ghosts over my lips.

"I've loved you for a long time, Andy," he murmurs. "And I know today is hell, this last week, but I need you to know. You don't have to say anything back, but I just—" He exhales, shaking his head. "I need you to know that I am here. I will always be here."

A fresh tear slides down my cheek. But this time, it's not from grief. It's from everything else.

Because somehow, in all this mess...

I ended up with him. The one person who sees every broken piece of me and doesn't turn away. I cup his face. Pressing my lips against his. Slow. Aching.

When I pull back, I don't hesitate. "I love you too."

His breath shudders, and then he kisses me, slowly and deep, like he's sealing those words into my skin.

When he pulls away, his fingers brush through my hair.

"Come on, beautiful. Let's go inside."

I nod, letting him lead me back in, and for the first time, maybe ever, I know.

I'm exactly where I'm supposed to be.

Epilogue

Andy

I didn't expect life to change this fast after graduation. But it has.

Change isn't just something I have to adjust to anymore.

It's something I want. Something I need.

The dorms feel different, not just for me, but for everyone. Alex and I have grown even closer, spending as much free time together as we can, but also having more social time with our family and friends. The dorms are a bustle of relationships forming and friendships growing.

But it's not all sunshine and rainbows. Despite having our family safe, Roarke's still too tense, like he's waiting for the other shoe to drop. Alex and Riddick have tried to get him to open up, but he avoids it. Focused instead on missions and training.

We spend more time at home, which is good for my sisters. My mom is finally coming out of her shell. She and I have talked about the books I got for her. I also know Maria, Sarah and the rest have been stopping by. Checking on her. She has even talked about getting a job at the library on campus.

Roarke and Mya's relationship is still strained. I tried talking to both, but Mya is a closed book, and Roarke just walks away whenever her name is mentioned. Mya is constantly in the training rooms and the boot, throwing herself into combat prep and mission readiness like her life depends on it.

And then there's Mason. Who is thriving under the attention she pretends she doesn't want.

It's been a while, but the whole Riddick, Bastian, and Kyle battle for her affections is back alive again.

If anything, with the ban lifted, it's getting worse.

Riddick isn't giving up. Being her main combat partner helps his case.

But Bastian? He's got the Tier Two connection, collaborating with her daily on trainings and enhancements for the Gen Fours and Fives.

If anything, he's doubling down, pushing Mason's buttons every day. Alex says that it's not romantic, but I don't know. Part of me wonders if he isn't contemplating making a proper move for her.

And Kyle?

Kyle's watching. Waiting. Like he knows something the others don't.

It's a beautiful disaster. And not my problem.

Because I've got one of my own. Alex. And his absolute lack of enthusiasm about the off-campus night, Kate and the social committee got approved.

I shift onto his lap, straddling him on the couch in our common room. "One night off campus won't kill you."

Alex exhales, rolling his eyes at me. "You're acting like this is a normal social event. It's not. It's a logistical nightmare."

"It's not just a night, Alex. It's the first night. The first time we're allowed to just…. Be. No escorts. No check-ins. Just music and drinks, a night that belongs to us. Besides, it's a controlled event. We've arranged security, transportation, and prevented anyone from going rogue."

His jaw ticks. I grin, pressing a kiss to his jaw. "You are jealous."

"Not jealous." He grumbles. "Just aware."

I smirk, letting my lips skim down his throat. "Jealous."

His fingers tighten on my waist. "Keep teasing me," he murmurs, voice low, dangerous, "but you love that I'm possessive."

I shiver. "Never said I didn't."

He flips me, pinning me against the couch, his hands bracing against the cushions. His weight presses into me, solid and certain.

"I don't like it," he admits, his voice quiet but firm. "Too many variables. Too many risks."

Alex

I fucking hate the idea of this off-campus event.

It's not just about the security risks—though, yeah, that's a huge part of it. It's that this is the first real freedom most of these guys and girls have had, and they will take full advantage of it.

I can only imagine what happens when you throw a bunch of high-powered, high-energy, formerly restricted soldiers into a normal setting.

It's a disaster waiting to happen.

And Andy? She is excited.

It means that despite everything screaming that this is a bad idea, we're going to the event.

Even if I hate every damn second of it.

But then there's her, warm, real, laughing against my chest, and I forget to stay mad.

She's teasing me, nudging at my defenses, trying to make me jealous just for fun.

She's right. I am jealous. Not because I don't trust her. I could say it. That I hate every eye on her. That she's mine.

But I whisper something quieter. Sharper. "One night is all it takes."

She stills. Not from surprise, but because she understands. The reminder. She was taken from me once. I won't let it happen again.

She cups my face, her eyes soft, knowing. "I'm not going anywhere."

I breathe her in, pressing my forehead to hers. "I know."

I don't want to release her, but I know that holding her too tight—keeping her caged—isn't what she needs.

What we need.

"I love you," she whispers, her fingers tangling in my hair.

I tighten my hold, pressing a slow, deep kiss to her lips. "I love you too."

This is ours.

Wherever she goes. Whatever happens.

I'll be by her side. And I'll protect her. Always.

Even if I can't predict what this night brings...

I'll survive it. And so will she.

Because she's mine—and I'm not letting go.

About the Author

S.H. Reynolds is an indie author, who writes emotionally charged, character-driven stories that blend romance, suspense, found family, with fierce heroines, and morally grey heroes.

Her books blend sarcasm, banter, and found family vibes to make you want to immerse yourself in their world.

An avid reader all her life, she recently got back into writing after a hiatus to raise a family. Her debut series, The Elitus Saga, explores the dark side of genetic engineering, military control, and what it means to fight for your own future.

When she's not writing, S.H. Reynolds can be found working a 9-5, lost in a good book, spending time with her family, or being a dedicated crazy cat lady.

Follow S.H. Reynolds on her Social Media
Goodreads: SHReynolds_author
TikTok:@SHreynoldsauthor
FB :@S.H. Reynolds Author
Pinterest: @SHReynoldsauthor
Amazon Author: S.H. Reynolds